The Persistent Marquess

by

Susan Payne

This is a work of fiction. Names, characters, places, and incidents are either the product of the author's imagination or are used fictitiously, and any resemblance to actual persons living or dead, business establishments, events, or locales, is entirely coincidental.

The Persistent Marquess

COPYRIGHT © 2020 by Susan Kay Payne

The Wild Rose Press, Inc.
PO Box 708
Adams Basin, NY 14410-0708
Visit us at www.thewildrosepress.com

Publishing History
First Line Rose Edition, 2020
Trade Paperback Print ISBN 978-1-5092-3223-9
Digital ISBN 978-1-5092-3224-6

Published in the United States of America

"Daisy, your grandmother and I agreed you needed to have the protection of my name once we were found on that balcony. I thought you realized the importance of such, as well."

"I recognized the fact my grandmother was distressed my name was linked with yours and that her society, her friends, felt I was ruined. I wanted to return home. Some days that is still my sole desire."

"You cannot mean that. You said your parents were so involved with one another you felt as if you were an interloper. Soon they will have a young child to care for. How would you fit into the family then? Be reasonable, Daisy, think about your own marriage. What you owe me as your husband."

"My lord, since you are anxious to return to London before the end of the season, why not simply get right down to the work involved. Get me with child so you may be on your way and I will be doing what I must."

It was either contrariness or merely that he didn't like being told what to do, but William balked at his wife's orders. "We are not breeding stock. There usually is some sort of compatibility between the couple involved, the sharing of lives, and then the begetting of children."

"I think I was very honest with you, my lord. I told you what I needed in a marriage. I wanted personal consideration, love, devotion. I must settle with much less than that and I cannot see why you should think to get everything you wanted. I will bare you children, whenever and how many you beget unto me. Pretending anything else, I believe, will cause us both to become too jaded to be decent to one another. I will await your pleasure…."

Praise for Susan Payne

A New Face in Town "Once again Susan Payne brings her gift for creating multi-layered characters, colloquial dialogue, and describing rich settings…"~ *Kat Henry Doran, Wild Women Reviews*

Dedication

To my lovely daughters for their support and long hours of Beta reading. May you always have love in your lives.

Other Stories by Susan Payne

Harrison Ranch & Macgregor's Mail Order Bride
Sweetwater Series, Book One

A Midwife for Sweetwater & A New Face in Town
Sweetwater Series, Book Two

Jeremy's Home & There's Always Hope
Sweetwater Series, Book Three

New Banker in Town & Happy Endings
Sweetwater Series, Book Four

London 1821

CHAPTER ONE

The Marquess of Ashton tried to hide the yawn behind his hand, but knew he wasn't going to fool any of his friends he ran into. Many of whom were with him last evening and knew exactly what he had been up to and when he had finally finished doing it. He knew it was too early to leave since he had just made his way through his cousin's receiving line. And beginning a game of cards this early in the night, with his head still fuzzy from all the drink of the evening before, was not a good idea. Evidently some part of his brain was still functioning if he could reason that much.

Casually gazing over the crowded ballroom, he nonchalantly moved closer to the wall with the closed French doors. His luck was with him as usual. He knew one more furtive step would have him well hidden behind the potted palm that had been his conspirator through so many of these damnable functions.

As he took that last step, still making sure no one noticed his actions, he bumped into something or, rather, someone who was never there before. Turning in surprise, he saw a pretty, auburn-haired young woman wearing the required demure, pastel gown of a lady in her first season. Although she was too young for his taste, her gaze held his with their unusual violet color.

William was forced to ask, even though they had never been introduced, "Why in the world are you hiding

Susan Payne

behind this palm? You are more than attractive enough to get any young man in this room wanting to partner you. So why are you hiding?" He took this time to examine the young lady and reached the same conclusion as before – attractive, very attractive, in an ingénue fashion.

On the attack, the young lady replied, "I could ask you the same question, my lord. After all, I found this hiding place first."

His own sense of the ridiculous came to his aid and he smiled, replying as eloquently as he would if speaking in front of the House of Lords.

"Although I hate to argue with a lady, I must disagree as to you being here first. I have always used this particular potted palm as a cover when enjoying an event at the Duke of Westland's home. And I have never run into you before, ergo, it was mine first."

Defeated by his logic, the young woman went to step-out from behind the palm and give up her refuge.

His hand grabbed her arm as he hissed, "Not now. That is the Duchess of Kirkland and one of the biggest gossips in town. If you slide out from behind this palm now, she will have it all over town we were back here together. And I do not plan on facing an angry papa in the morning on the field of honor."

"My papa isn't even in town and he is too busy caring for Mama to worry about my good name," she replied sounding chagrined.

"Does that have anything to do with why you are hiding back here?" William's sympathies stirred for the young woman who seemingly didn't want to be at this ball any more than he did.

"My mother is *enceinte'* and I must live with the

snickers from the gentlemen and the rolling of eyes and whispers from the young ladies of the ton. And that is nothing compared to what their mothers are saying. Evidently, couples my parent's age are too old for such things and everyone is aghast that Mama has the gall to become in the family way. And that the child is my father's potential heir has fanned the fires of scandal even more."

The hem of her dress brushed the top of his dance shoes due to their enforced proximity he was sure.

The young woman turned her violet eyes up to his and confided quietly, "I think she would have been thought better of by the tabbies if the child were a lover's rather than my father's. As if having an affair were more acceptable than still making love to one's own husband. Is that how it is with the ton?"

William made sure he was still awake and this forward young woman was actually speaking these things to him. She seemed to expect a reply. He wasn't sure he should comment or merely let the chit leave with all her questions unanswered.

Because she appeared so serious and against his better sense, he answered, "I think it very inspiring to know that any marriage could continue for such a time and the couple remain faithful and loving towards one another. You should put all the gossipmongers where they belong - out of your mind. Do not let them turn something so poignantly beautiful into compelling you to hide yourself away instead of enjoying your season."

The young lady stood a little taller although that was not much over five-foot-two-inches as she nodded her head. "I agree. I am proud of my parents and I should be proud that I will have a new brother or sister come late fall. My parents have never shown anything but care and love for one another. If mama is still young enough to give me a sibling, then I should be grateful and stare down those who would besmirch her good name."

"That's the girl." He peered through the dense palm fronds and found the coast clear for her to depart unnoticed. "Ah, before you leave, should we at least introduce ourselves in case we run into one another on the street."

At the girl's hesitation over protocol, he continued, "I mean, we are co-conspirators at this point and we should at least be able to put a name with a face."

He introduced himself bowing as if being presented to a debutante by the girl's chaperon. "May I introduce myself, the Marquess of Ashton, at your service. After our interlude this evening feel free to call me, Ashton, or think of me as, William."

Smiling shyly, the young woman curtsied appropriately. "So, pleased to meet you, my lord. I am Miss Daisy Vincent. My father is Viscount Weatherly and my mother is…."

"With child…I think that has been covered." For some reason this young woman's story warmed his heart and gave him a meager hope for the future. Not his but others' future. Those of his married friends.

"I wish them all the best," he said after she rose to her full height once more.

"I know I should be embarrassed at having confessed all of this to you, my lord. Has anyone told you that you are a very good listener?" She blushed, saying without guile, "I have been told I am too trusting and I do not know the proper way to go about in society. That is why my parents insisted I come to London for my season even though all sorts of things are occurring back home."

"And back home is where?" William couldn't believe he was still speaking with this young woman, as if who and what she was mattered to him. He shook his head to clear the fog that seemed to act as a cloud over his judgement. He decided to send her out – out of the hiding place, out of his presence and out of his life. He did not need complications that a young debutante could cause.

"Home is in Sussex, but I am staying with my grandmother, Lady Reynolds, for the season. And at this rate, I will not return after the Christmas holiday."

Knowing he was embroiling himself even further into her life, he couldn't prevent the words. "Why is that, Miss Vincent?"

"Although you have been more than kind about my predicament, others do not seem so compassionate. Not that worry over such things, but my grandmother is mortified by the talk and can hardly bring herself to face her friends. I think it so unfair. I almost wish to do something extreme and be sent home in disgrace. Then I can be with my parents and help take care of the new baby when he arrives."

The talk of ruining herself warned William again of how truly inappropriate his hiding away with her behind his fern has been.

"I look forward to meeting you again, Miss Vincent. Perhaps in Hyde Park some afternoon? Until then." He bowed and motioned with his head for her to slip out when the dance ended and there were people moving off and onto the dance floor.

Concealed, he watched his young cohort as she

made her way to the other side of the room mostly behind the backs of those watching the set being filled. She approached an older dowager and settled close to that lady's side. He could see the older woman smile weakly and then look furtively around to see if her friends noticed her protégé's return.

And they did - many actually turning away and tittering behind their fans to one another. William never held a high opinion of the matchmaking mamas, but this was a bit ludicrous to ridicule a young woman because her parents were still enjoying one another after twenty-plus years of marriage. If her mother was young enough to conceive then she was still young enough to be making love, especially with her own husband.

The more he thought about Miss Vincent's dilemma, the more he realized he was probably not much younger than her parents. At least her mother, who may have married an older man, which was certainly not unknown in the ton.

William at two and thirty was just entering his prime and still not wed. If the tabbies thought the viscountess too old to still be bedded by her husband, what would they think of him when he finally began his nursery?

He knew it was different for a man, but he didn't wish to be dealing with debutantes when he decided to wed. Possibly an older widow or would that still raise eyebrows and cause rude comments? He did not like the way people felt the need to infringe on other's lives and he did not like the way the so-called ladies of the ton were keeping the young men away from Miss Vincent.

Daisy kept smiling as if having the best time at her first ball. She tried to talk to her grandmother about the lovely dresses and how well the orchestra played, but that good lady was unable to pay any attention to her granddaughter.

Willing to leave early, Daisy said, "Grandmother, I know you wanted this to be a long night as we prepared for it, but I think we have done justice to the evening. I have been seen as attending and that is all we wished to accomplish, wasn't it?" Then continued without thinking, "I mean I am relatively unknown to London and I did not expect to fill my dance card."

The comment did not sit well with Lady Reynolds as her mouth began to tremble and her eyes filled with mist. Just then a dark hulk strode-up smoothly and bowed to the older lady before making a comment to both women.

"Lady Reynolds, please excuse the impropriety of this introduction. I am, Marquess of Ashton."

Daisy watched fascinated as that lady simply nodded in wonderment at having this paragon of the ton speaking with her for whatever reason, causing her to blush with pride.

He continued, "I am so glad to have met up with you. Miss Vincent's father, the viscount, wanted me to be sure to make myself known to you while in London."

Suddenly realizing all eyes were upon them, Lady Reynolds smiled and held out her hand as she remembered her duty and took the opportunity of introducing her granddaughter to the marquess.

"This is my granddaughter the Honorable Daisy Vincent." Daisy went into a curtsy as if she had not just done so a little while earlier behind the palm.

Bowing over her hand, William said suavely, "Charmed, Miss Vincent." Turning back to her grandmother, he continued, "Do you mind if I ask a dance of Miss Vincent? I presumed upon your favor and have been given permission she be allowed to waltz. It is the only dance I do competently and I feel as if I know Miss Vincent so well, being acquainted with her parents as I am."

"Of course, of course, my lord." Lady Reynolds beamed with pride. She was now able to look anyone in the eye close enough to be paying attention to her granddaughter's conquest. Those people, the women especially, appeared jealous as the marquess led Daisy out to the dance floor.

As the marquess must have planned, the dance was a waltz and he did not hesitate to stand in front of Daisy and place his gloved hand upon her back, his arms long enough to make sure the proper distance was kept between them. The music began and Daisy stepped with him as if they had practiced the dance numerous times together.

Daisy was enjoying her partner twirling her so proficiently in the dance. She showed her appreciation with a bright smile which she hoped he knew was only for him. Feeling grateful, pleasure, and pride they whirled with the other dancers. As the music came to an end, he bowed to her curtsy. The marquess escorted Daisy off the floor and back to her grandmother who was still where they left her. Only this time surrounded by many of the same woman who had been ignoring her all evening.

Lord Ashton didn't stay to be introduced, much to the ladies' disappointment. After he left, other young men approached Lady Reynolds to ask for the opportunity to dance with Daisy. They were all accepted until her dance card was filled and those young men who did not have a dance stood nearby to speak with her between dance partners.

Neither Daisy nor her grandmother saw the marquess after that dance. Daisy knew the lord had asked for the dance simply to put the other ladies' noses out of joint, as her father would have said. The viscount would have said a lot more if he had seen how Daisy and his mother-by-marriage had been treated by the ton tonight. It was as well her parents had decided to stay in the country rather than chance her mother's health in the soot-filled city air.

Daisy and her grandmother both wore smiles on their faces while riding home from the Westland's ball in their carriage. She didn't want the exhilaration of her first ball to be diminished by anything. Neither mentioned the abrupt change in the ton's attitude part way through the party and neither mentioned the cause of it.

She was glad because she didn't feel like she could lie about how she really met the marquess and that he didn't know her parents either. At least, not before she told him of her dilemma. And that dilemma seemed to have disappeared as soon as the marquess made himself known to the ton as having an interest in Daisy and her grandmother.

CHAPTER TWO

Daisy, with her grandmother in attendance, found herself at home the next day entertaining several of the other debutantes and their mothers who attended the Westland's ball. Daisy found she liked several of the young ladies and was once more grateful for the marquess' intervention the evening before. Coming to her rescue like some knight from King Arthur's Court.

The formal parlor was filled with chairs brought in from other rooms to give their guests enough seats. The tables covered with plates and tea cups could barely be distinguished. Only the framed oil paintings and mirror on the wall appeared familiar.

One of the mothers, having her second cup of tea, finally broached the question evidently on all the visitors' minds. "Lady Reynolds, is the Marquess of Ashton expected this afternoon?"

That fine lady smiled conspiratorially. "Well, the marquess did not specify an exact date. Merely that he hoped to visit my granddaughter and I some time in the near future. I welcome his visit at any point, of course, since he is friends with Daisy's father, Viscount Weatherly."

Daisy felt herself flush knowing her grandmother was propagating the fabrication that the marquess began. But Daisy wasn't able to correct her for fear her grandmother would wonder why the marquess would have begun such a fairytale to begin with. The fact Daisy tried hiding behind that blasted palm would come out and then her grandmother would once more feel the humiliation of the ton's disapproval. It was simply better to smile and assume that everything her grandmother said was gospel.

One of the youngest debutantes, Lady Alice Wainwright, the only daughter of an earl, turned to Daisy saying, "My brother and a few friends are going for a ride in the park tomorrow afternoon. Would you be available to make a party of it with us?"

Daisy glanced toward her grandmother who was busy speaking with one of the matrons, so answered, "I am sure it will be fine with my grandmother. She rarely goes out except for afternoon visits with friends and then seldom more than once a week. Most of her friends are elderly and tend to fall asleep in the afternoon."

"That is perfect because my mother thinks if I am around you, my chance of meeting the marquess will be ensured. And while I thought him very handsome, he was also very frightening. If you are with me on outings, then Mamma will be content and you can be a buffer between the marquess and myself since you seem to be able to handle his attention. I, on the other hand, do not wish to even speak with him."

She looked slightly worried and asked, "Was that too blunt? Mamma says I am too honest or forthright or some such similar words and that I must not be so brash. Yes, that is the word she used this morning, that I must not be brash. Was I? Brash, I mean, just now?"

"No, I do not feel so. I think you were being honest and I am one to be thought to be honest, too. So if it is a fault, I am afraid we both must suffer from it." Daisy confided to her new friend.

"Well, then that is as it should be. I would like at

least one friend I can depend on to let me know when I might be putting a foot wrong without raking me over the coals. It seems that having a season is full of pitfalls and one must be careful or one can trip and be trampled by the others." She glanced around to see if anyone was paying any mind to them before whispering, "My brother, who is older by a couple of years, says he will protect me as much as he is able, but his friends can only do so much and then I am on my own."

"The two of us can be on our own together. Two of us must be stronger than either one of us alone. I will be ready tomorrow about three if that is all right for our ride. We can make more plans to meet then."

"That will be wonderful. Oh, Mamma is getting ready to leave. I am so glad she brought me here today. I just know we will be best of friends."

Daisy saw her new confidante and her mother out and returned to the room to find other mothers with daughters leaving to make another call or depart for home to receive any late callers of their own now that the marquess proved he wasn't going to make a show.

The next afternoon, Daisy was ready and waiting in the foyer when the footman opened the door to a young man who bowed over her hand and introduced himself easily.

"Lord Terrill, at your service, Miss Vincent. My sister, Lady Alice, is in the carriage with a couple of others. Are you ready?"

"Certainly, I appreciate that you are taking time out of your day to escort me this afternoon. My grandmother only has one of those large older coaches which one cannot take a ride through Hyde Park in, no matter how much one wishes to," Daisy explained as she went out to the open barouche filled with other young people and allowed Lord Terrill to hand her up the step.

Alice did the introductions from there and the group was off for an entertaining day in the park. Evidently seeing and being seen the main purpose of any such outing.

Daisy returned flushed from the fun and sun of the outing and could not stop talking about it to her grandmother all through dinner and afterward. She described hats some of the women were sporting and the fine-looking horses and equipage others rode in.

"Daisy, dear, please do not use street cant when speaking of horses. It makes a young lady seem so fresh and that is not a good thing, believe me. One must be reserved and have the utmost decorum whenever one is in public and that includes in your own home. You are always within sight or hearing of others and how they view you is how the world views you," her grandmother admonished.

"Yes, Grandmother, I understand and am deeply sorry if I showed less than modest enthusiasm for what I saw today. And for the new friends I met," Daisy told that lady sincerely.

Lady Reynolds patted her hand saying, "That is all right, my dear. I really am glad you have made friends among your own age. I am not so senile I do not realize the Marquess of Ashton was merely being nice to you because he is a friend of your father. After all, he is so much above us we should be thankful for his acknowledgement at the ball. That is all we should expect and the rest will be up to us."

"I understand, Grandmother, and I would never presume upon the marquess for any further aid. As you say, he is so much above us."

Daisy believed everything she told her grandmother and was well entrenched with Alice and her brother, James, as well as several of their friends when she once more encountered the marquess, only this time she was in the carriage with Alice and several young men.

As they passed through the park's gate, the carriages all seemed to come to a standstill. The marquess was exiting on a large roan. The horse's size equal to the size of the man riding it. Daisy felt her cheeks flush when she saw him. The marquess, unable to stop, tipped his hat in acknowledgement, which made Daisy color even more, the heat of her face almost beyond tolerable.

Alice leaned over and giggled, "He saw you. He saw you. Did you see him?"

"Yes, I saw him, Alice. Now can we simply forget it and move on?" Daisy urged as the young men in the carriage looked upon her with new interest, even James. Daisy could not believe that the slightest nod from a marquess would raise her in other's estimation. Was the ton so shallow then? Were her new friends so shallow, also?

Two days later, as the group drove through the park on an exceedingly warm day, Daisy saw the marquess on the same roan horse. She prevented herself from ducking beneath the side of the carriage so she wouldn't be seen and have attention drawn to herself.

She inwardly cringed when she noticed the marquess rein in his horse and head toward the barouche in which she and her friends were riding. Politeness dictated she acknowledge his approach and that she introduces her friends if he stopped and indicated he wished to make their acquaintance. And he did.

"Miss Vincent, how nice to find you riding in the fresh air today."

"Yes, my lord, it is a very fine day for a ride." He looked expectantly at the others in the open carriage.

"May I introduce you to my companions? My good friend, Lady Alice Wainwright, and her brother, Lord Terrill. Then there is Lord Jarvis, Viscount Headley and Mister Lister," she introduced trying not to stammer in the marquess' presence.

The marquess bowed his head politely to Alice saying, "Lady Alice. Gentlemen. I won't keep you standing, the horses get so restless in this heat. I hope you enjoy your ride, ladies. Gentlemen." He nodded in farewell and turned his horse to canter towards the gate.

Everyone in the carriage was silent for a moment and then they all began to speak as if some sort of spell had been cast off.

Mister Lister said excitedly "I say, that horse is a splendid animal, what?"

"And did you get a look at his boots? Amazing workmanship. I wish I knew where he got them. Mine are sadly out of date, I fear," Lord Jarvis complained eyeing the high polished Hessians on his feet.

Alice and her brother simply stared at Daisy who couldn't think of anything to say to explain the marquess selecting their carriage to acknowledge. She merely smiled tightly, hoping no one would ask any embarrassing questions.

Daisy was quiet for the rest of the ride. The others having forgotten the marquess as they met and talked with acquaintances out to enjoy the sunny afternoon, as well.

The group ended their trip with a stop at Günter's

Teashop for ices and James ordered for all of them from the waiters who came out to the curb. By then, even Daisy had stopped worrying about the marquess and his effect on her friends. It was a simple, accidental meeting and no one would think any more of it after today.

James walked Daisy to her door as usual after one of the outings and said, "Do you plan on attending the Guthrie's ball this Friday evening?"

"Yes, I believe my grandmother sent in our acceptance last week."

"I would like the first and supper dances if that is acceptable to you," he said seriously which was unusual for him. He was the one who kept them all laughing at his imitation of his tutors and headmaster while he was at school. Often mimicking public figures and making a political statement at the same time.

"Certainly, James, I will write your name in those lines as soon as I receive my card," Daisy said smiling and thinking that perhaps this season would not end as badly as she first feared.

"Then I look forward to seeing you at the Guthrie's," James said as he backed towards the carriage, not taking his gaze off her as she entered her home.

Daisy was anxious to get through the receiving line and onto the dance floor so James could find her in time for the first dance. She had hurried so Grandmother and her could find a place along the sidelines and watch as the rest of the guests descended to the ballroom. That way, Daisy would know when James arrived but the line was moving ever so slowly.

Lady Reynolds stood serene and calm, finally telling her granddaughter sotto voice, "Daisy, you must stop fidgeting or others will think there is something wrong with your wardrobe. You know, like your slips are hanging or some such."

"I am sorry, Grandmother, I will try to have more decorum. It is only that I have promised the first dance to Lord Terrell, Alice's brother, and I do not wish to disappoint him," Daisy explained as they approached the Guthries welcoming their guests.

"I do not think the music will start with so many people yet to be greeted, my dear, so you can relax and meet your hosts with a warm smile as a young lady should."

"Certainly, Grandmother, I was worried over nothing. I could just as well have danced the second dance with James instead. It is not as if my card has anyone else on it yet," Daisy said reasonably.

The Guthries was the first ball Lady Reynolds and Daisy received an invitation to since the Duke of Westland's two-weeks previously. Although the number of invitations to all sorts of amusements doubled on the salver since the marquess made his introduction, it wasn't a bountiful number considering how many entertainments occurred nightly.

Lady Reynolds accepted a place near a small sofa where she could talk with other older guests and watch Daisy and her friends as a companion should.

James stood beside Daisy as soon as she arrived and greeted Alice. The three were joined by Alice's first partner, Mister Lister, and then, Lord Jarvis. The music began and Daisy looked shyly toward James as he smiled taking her hand on his arm to lead her out to the center of the dance floor.

The dance ended and Daisy's cheeks felt warm from

the exertion of the quadrille and she returned to the side of the dance floor where her next partner, Lord Jarvis, was already waiting for the second dance.

Lord Norris took his dance by allowing Daisy to rest while he went to get her some refreshment. Standing alone, watching all her friends dancing, the marquess approached her while every eye watched, including many of the dancers on the floor.

"Miss Vincent, you look lovely this evening. May I have this dance?"

She curtsied upon his arrival. "I appreciate the honor, my lord, but I am already slated with Lord Norris. He is retrieving a lemonade for me as I am so parched. I am afraid that my card is filled. I would have saved you a dance if I had known you would be attending tonight."

Lord Ashton made an unusual tip of his head and gave a slight bow saying, "Perhaps another time, then."

William stood to the far side of the ballroom and thought, well, she showed me what she thought of me, or rather, what I thought of myself. Any other young lady in her position would have eagerly accepted my request and be damned to the man's name that was written on her dance card. He chuckled at his own loss of self-importance.

Daisy, that sweet, honest young lady truthfully told him she did not have an opening on her card. At this very moment, she was probably dancing with some vicar's son in what could have been William's dance if she were a different sort of female. But then he wouldn't find her as fascinating. She would be like all the other debutantes at all the other balls he attended and departed early from, disappointed in the offerings of another season.

But this time, this time he couldn't stop watching her. Daisy, even her name was refreshing, like springtime, like a renewal for his too jaded mind.

His gaze caught the swirl of her dress as she was partnered in a waltz that could have been his if only he had let her know he was going to be here tonight. She had said the words to him innocent of flirtation or guile.

Smiling to himself, he turned to get his hat. He would take this memory with him and hopefully, next time, plan ahead to let her know he was going to be attending a ball.

CHAPTER THREE

Daisy and Alice were shopping for new ribbons so Daisy could make a dress she had already worn twice appear different while Alice swore, she needed another bonnet although she wasn't sure which dress it would need to go with. The two young ladies were head to head, comparing the rose hues of the ribbons when they heard an older woman say Lord Ashton's name.

Both friends stopped talking immediately. Daisy tried to ignore the following gossip but Alice, intrigued, held up her hand to shush Daisy and Alice leaned toward the speaker.

"I heard it myself. My husband said that Lord Ashton was setting his cap for one of this year's debutantes and there was a betting book at Whites the other members of the ton kept track of the wagers in." The matron sounded as if she knew what she was talking about. A reliable source for sure.

The second unknown woman stated, "Why that is simply outrageous. Some poor girl's name is going to be tarnished just for being a possible contender for this so-called honor? It is a travesty such things are allowed to occur among decent families."

The first woman continued, "Not only that, but there are at least three debutantes, all right out of the school room, who are leading the pack as far as possibilities. All closely related to a duke, no less."

"Well, of course a marquess wouldn't think to wed much lower than a duke's daughter. After all, he could hardly choose a mere Earl's prodigy, now could he?"

"Or a mere baron's so that leaves out your daughter as well, Cynthia."

"Do not be cruel, Agatha, it does not become you. You can be mean-spirited because you never had a daughter you must get married off. It is not as easy as a son believe you me. Now my son will have several young ladies to choose from, even if he will only be a baron one day. At least it is a title and comes with a tidy income as well."

"I am sorry if I hurt your feelings, Cynthia, please forgive my poor judgment. I am sure your daughter could capture the marquess' eye if she tried."

"Don't be a fool, Agatha. My daughter will be lucky if she catches the eye of the fishmonger. The poor thing looks so much like her father I almost weep every time I see her."

Then the women's voices faded away as they moved further into the shop and disappeared behind the dressing room curtain.

Alice, her large blue eyes wider than Daisy had ever seen them asked, "Did you hear all of that? Your marquess is going to marry a duke's daughter and he actually stopped and greeted you in Hyde Park one afternoon. How exciting that is."

"I found those two women totally insensitive. What if one of those 'duke's daughters' had been here instead of us. They would have been mortified, completely devastated their name was being bandied about like that. And written in the betting books as well. How horrible for them."

"I find the news terribly interesting. I mean, do you think we could find out who he is interested in and then place a bet ourselves? Well, not ourselves exactly but James could place a bet for us. Why should the men have all the chances to bet on this when we have access to first-hand information? You can ask Lord Ashton who he prefers the next time you see him."

"Alice, did you not hear what I just said. Those poor girls are going to be fodder for every lout that places a bet. You must think it is very bad ton to do something so vile. I mean, what about the girls who do not get the ring? They would have been smeared by the mere fact their names were put up as a possibility."

"But Daisy, they are the daughters of dukes. How much damage can they receive with their fathers' power and money protecting them?"

"I think you have been around your brother and his friends too much if you really think I would use my acquaintanceship with the marquess to help your brother win a bet that should never be made."

"You're right, Daisy, I merely thought it would be nice to win a bet when there wouldn't be a chance of losing. I did not really think it through as far as the young ladies were concerned. The two not chosen are going to be considered losers no matter how it turns out, but that does not mean we should participate in their downfall," Alice said sincerely.

"I am sure you would have figured out the right thing to do for yourself once you thought it through. I mean, even those matrons were not very concerned with the reputations of the young ladies involved. If we were more socially connected, we could probably guess which debutantes were being discussed and then we would feel obligated to inform their parents. I am glad I do not have the barest idea of who these poor girls might be."

Daisy paid for the length of ribbon she selected and left the shop without ever seeing either of the women who had gotten her so off-balance. Hearing the marquess' name bandied about was a little unsettling, but to hear his name linked to those of possible wives made everything seem to swim in front of her eyes for a moment. She was sure it was because she thought it so unfair to the three debutantes. Possibly because she had faced such ridicule when she first entered London's society.

Although she tried to ignore her thoughts, Daisy still felt slightly ill and declined dinner altogether after not being able to have more than a cup at afternoon tea. She pled to having a headache and retired early so her grandmother could not question her too much about being disheartened.

Lying in bed did not bring relief and it did not bring sleep. She tossed and turned without really knowing what or rather who was disturbing her usual easy rest. Was she angry at the women who talked so freely in a public place? The men at Whites who would take and make bets on a young woman's future? At the marquess for putting himself and the ladies he favored in the center of a target for others to take aim at? Or for herself since she could not stop thinking about the marquess or his future bride, whoever she may be.

Daylight was breaking before exhaustion finally brought her sleep, but it was not peaceful and she woke grumpy and mad at the world.

Daisy was finally feeling less fragile and more like her old self. It had taken several days but after attending evening events with her grandmother and not hearing anything more about Lord Ashton's future intended, she relaxed. Thinking the two women she and Alice heard talking were wrong and that the marquess wasn't actually hunting for a wife more this year than any other.

As she was sitting at the pianoforte, playing a long-loved ballad, her grandmother's butler, Tuttle, brought her a note with a crested seal melted into the wax. She opened it rather excitedly since this was the first note such as this she had ever received. She opened the missive and read, 'Save me a dance, WB'.

She looked it over on both sides and other than her name on the outside, there was nothing else to indicate whom the note came from, but of course, she knew. She had told the marquess she would save him a dance if she knew he would be attending a ball. So, this was her request for a dance, in advance, for the ball at the Dandales she was planning to attend that evening.

Her first impulse was to send a note back telling him her dance card was full, but then realized that would be considered too rude, even for her. After all, Lord Ashton really didn't have any responsibility as to what the peers bet on at Whites or anywhere else. She was sure he didn't have anything to do with it.

Except for possibly telling someone he had three candidates and would be making up his mind by the end of the season, Lord Ashton was innocent. His actions completely above board and nothing more than conjecture. The ton surmising the possibility of his marriage by his attendance at more events this season than past ones.

Now who was listening to gossip? Daisy found out that tidbit of information from Alice who heard it from her own mother. Evidently, following the comings and goings of marquess was fair game and the same went for dukes and their daughters, evidently.

Daisy felt a little nervous entering the ballroom as her grandmother found a chair to sit in along one of the walls with the other elderly companions. Daisy searched out Alice and her brother James. James asked for the first dance again this evening as well as the supper dance which was beginning to become a habit although they always sat together as a group with Alice, Lord Jarvis, Viscount Headley, and Mister Lister.

She tried to pay attention to the others, their talk of attending a race at the edge of London where a track was being built. Daisy found she was unable to listen and remained attuned to a tall dark-haired man approaching her.

Brushing her hand down the lavender skirts of her gown she affirmed it was the best selection for tonight. She knew it went well with her eyes and flattered her figure. She even thought, she appeared taller when she wore a gown with a scooped neckline and puff sleeves. Possibly she was giving the dress magical properties it did not possess, but feeling attractive was as good as being attractive her grandmother told her. Tonight, she felt attractive wearing this gown.

She wasn't sure if the marquess simply expected her to write his name at any open dance or if he wished a particular one. Knowing he waltzed, Daisy placed his name in both slots in case he did not arrive by the first waltz. She didn't wish to face him again and need to tell him her dance card was full. She felt terrible about having to do so last time and she could not come up with a reason why.

Daisy was on the dance floor when she saw the

marquess speaking with her grandmother, the elderly lady rosy cheeked with Lord Ashton's polite attention. He was watching for her, though, and at the end of the dance, she asked to be escorted to her grandmother's side.

There were a couple of moments of small talk as the orchestra tuned up for the first waltz and Lord Ashton turned to Daisy.

"Miss Vincent, I believe this dance is mine?"

Daisy replied with a smile and curtsy, "Why yes, I believe it is, my lord."

Then she placed her hand on his arm as he led her to the dance floor. Once more he stood in front of her. A very properly placed gloved hand on her back as he accepted her gloved hand in the other, keeping their bodies strictly separated.

The music swelled to a start and the first step was taken. Just as the first time, they were in tune with one another, his stride shortened to match her much smaller ones as they twirled and turned around the dance floor. Many eyes watched with speculation and curiosity.

Daisy tried not to notice. She was lost to the music and the dance and the man. She did not think of the possible future wife or duke's daughters or any of the things that had kept her awake that night days ago.

She simply gazed into his eyes and remembered their first dance together and how magical it felt for hours afterwards. How kind he had been when he found her hiding behind the palm, his palm he argued although he said he never argued with a lady. He was a man who always wanted control, who wanted to be right, who wanted to dance with a girl who was having trouble fitting in with the season's debutantes.

The music stopped and the couple that garnered more than their fair share of attention, bowed and curtsied and then he led Daisy properly back to her grandmother. Lord Ashton took his leave of Daisy and her grandmother, but not before leaning down and asking, "The second waltz has my name behind it, too, doesn't it?"

Daisy looked up startled and said, "Why yes, but...."

"That is all I need to know. I'll be back to claim you then." He bowed to both ladies and left before Daisy's next dance partner approached her.

Daisy spent the next several dances disconcerted. Worrying about what the marquess could possibly mean by dancing two dances with her when everyone knew he rarely danced even one per ball. What would people think?

What would her grandmother think? She certainly didn't want that poor lady to think something was happening between her granddaughter and the marquess. The disappointment when he chose his fiancée from the list of duke's daughters would be excruciating to watch. The ton might once again close ranks and shun her grandmother. Especially if Lady Reynolds made the error of saying anything that may be construed as linking Daisy and the marquess names.

Perhaps Daisy should tell her grandmother the gossip about the three duke's daughters. Forewarning Lady Reynolds so she didn't say something that would make them both look foolish come the day the marquess announced his betrothal to another debutante.

Daisy kept watching for Lord Ashton's return. Any tall, dark man among the companions would draw her attention, but she never saw him. Possibly he was in the cardroom and would become so involved with a game he would miss the second waltz. That hope died as she watched him walk toward her as she stood next to Alice and James. James noticed the tall man approaching as well and shot a look of hurt toward Daisy just before Lord Ashton claimed her for his dance.

For the second time that night, now with even more notice being taken of the couple, they took their place on the dance floor. Many eyebrows were raised in speculation and many fans covered whispered words to their neighbor's ear.

Raising her chin, she smiled while gazing into the blue eyes of her partner, noticing a slight hint of humor in them. He stood in front of her, placed his gloved hand on her back and took her gloved hand in his other and the music began. The magic that always went through her when he placed his hands on her began, also.

The twirling of partners commenced and the gossip, the stares, and the censuring looks all disappeared as she was swept up in the dance as always happened with her whenever she was in this man's arms. The music seemed to float around them, the people became a blur, and she focused on his face and his smile and his eyes, his very kind eyes with just that hint of humor.

She became aware that he was enjoying this dance as much as she was. He was feeling the music just as she was. He was watching her just as she was watching him.

As the music ended and the dancers came to a stop, many of them turned toward Daisy and the marquess as if they were setting the pace for the whole dance floor. Lord Ashton bowed as Daisy curtsied, he raised her and then placed her hand on his arm as he led her toward her friends.

However, that group were all agog, their eyes wide and a look of surprise still on most of their faces. Daisy stood primly among her friends as Lord Ashton took his leave once again. The crowd began to relax while conversations started up, the whispers stopped and partners reformed and made their way to the dance floor as the next set began.

Daisy stood smiling and watching as the lines formed and then the music began, and still Daisy didn't feel capable of speaking, of answering any questions she was afraid Alice was bursting to ask. However, Alice was now on the dance floor, leaving Daisy to watch her friends' performance serenely.

By the end of the dance, Daisy felt herself more capable of being sociable. More like her usual effervescent self.

Alice came back eagerly urging Daisy to move. "Come to the ladies' withdrawing room with me, Daisy. I think I tore the lace on my dress and I will need your help."

Daisy stopped herself from rolling her eyes at her friend's obvious ploy to get Daisy into a room where she could be grilled about that second Waltz. Daisy would forever think of this last dance in that way, with a capital - Waltz with Lord Ashton. The night Daisy realized he meant so much more to her than merely a nice man who was trying to make her season more pleasurable.

Daisy followed Alice as she was practically dragged to the room set aside for the ladies' use. Alice peered around the vacant room before she whispered conspiratorially, "Tell me what that was all about. I mean there is more between you two than simply a father's old friend being kind to you. What really is happening? Could he be seriously considering you as a wife?" This last was asked in awe, almost like a prayer.

It would take a prayer, rather many of them for her name to even make the list of candidates. And she could imagine her grandmother's shocked expression when she heard that her granddaughter's name had been added to the betting book at Whites. And the inevitable depression when her granddaughter wasn't chosen.

"No, do not even say such things even when we are alone. Do not even think such things, please for my sake. He is merely being kind. He is simply a friend of my father." Then she realized she thought of him as such for so long she was becoming immersed in the lie, too. "Lord Ashton will be mortified, I am sure, if he hears of any speculation between us. I mean, look at it realistically. I am so much younger than he is. I am a mere daughter of a viscount. I am simply an Honorable to his marquess. Please, do not think about us as any type of couple for then I could find myself being thought of with conjecture. You know how much damage that can do to anyone's reputation and I would be mortified if anyone mentioned it to Lord Ashton."

"Do you think anyone would be that daring?" Alice asked still with awe in her voice. "That someone would actually say something right to Lord Ashton's face?"

"It would take a brave person I assure you, but that would not stop those men at Whites from adding my name to the book. And that would put an end to my season. My grandmother would hear of it and she would never be able to go out in society again."

"Well, hopefully no one will do so. It just seems strange that he danced with you twice tonight and it was so, so.... I don't know, but your faces were...like closing the rest of us out. Like no one else existed besides the two of you and the music."

Daisy lowered her gaze when Alice described almost exactly the feeling Daisy herself felt when in Lord Ashton's arms. She would need to learn to hide her emotions more. What if the marquess saw Daisy's infatuation? How would she ever face the man again if she caused his name to be linked with that of a simple Miss?

A group of ladies came in, feigning surprise at finding Alice and Daisy in the room. Their speculative gazes taking in both young ladies and the lack of any one else in sight. Their minds could be seen spinning with questions and how to get the answers to them without seeming to be merely mining for information.

Daisy smiled benignly and walked out before the door closed from the women entering. Alice right behind her without allowing the new arrivals to say anything to either of them.

"Daisy, Daisy, where are you going?" panted Alice trying to keep up with her friend who was practically running.

"I need to get my grandmother and call for our carriage. I do not feel as if I can stay and be the center of contemplation any longer."

"If you leave it will be said that you ran from this ball after the dance and become more of an object of curiosity than you are right now. Stay and see the ball to its end. Chin up and head high and I will make sure you are not left on the side of the dance floor the rest of the evening."

"You are probably right. I do not wish to be seen as

if I was chased out by their glares and assumptions."
Daisy decided. "But I will go to my grandmother's side
before finding my next partner."

Lady Reynolds was sitting benignly on the sofa
talking with another woman of the same age, both
slightly surprised at her approach.

"Here is my granddaughter now. Lady Marley, let
me introduce the reason for my being at this event this
evening, my lovely granddaughter, the Honorable Daisy
Vincent."

"Oh, yes, she is as lovely as your daughter, is she
not? I am so glad to meet you, my dear. I first met your
mother when she was about your age, oh, too many years
ago. More than I wish to think about passing me by at
this time. Are you enjoying the dancing? You younger
generation seem to have so much stamina to keep going
all night long."

Daisy realized that neither woman was privy to what
had occurred on the dance floor, to the conjecture that
was now rife among the marriage-minded mammas.
Lady Reynolds let it be known that she was quite
comfortable on the sofa with her old friend. Daisy
curtsied and smiled and said the right things before her
grandmother sent her back to Alice and her other friends
for the rest of the evening.

Returned to her friends and true to her word, Alice
lined-up partners for every dance. Daisy never spent
more than a few minutes off the dance floor and so was
unavailable for anyone to speak with other than her next
dance partner. The evening went very well with this
pattern and soon the group was ready to depart to their
carriages.

Daisy collected her now drowsing grandmother

from the dwindling number of companions and took her home.

CHAPTER FOUR

The tea pot and cart had to be refilled several times to keep up with the steady stream of visitors who must have been lining-up outside Lady Reynold's residence the next day. Also, the butler and footman were kept busy accepting nosegays and handwritten sonnets from messengers dropping them off for Daisy.

Most of them were placed in the informal parlor so they didn't topple off the usual foyer table such things were set on. She didn't wish to think about the thank you notes she would need to send in response to all the missives. However, she thought it was better for people to send something than to show up and crowd the small receiving parlor even more.

Daisy was brought back to the present when Lady Gannon, the mother of a debutante who Daisy didn't even recognize, was saying to her grandmother, "But my lady, do you think that your granddaughter should be looking so high for a suitable match? I mean, she is a pretty girl and dances well, but she is simply not trained or prepared to become a marchioness."

This comment was overheard by everyone in the room, including a couple of the young men who were conversing with each other near the fireplace. All heads turned and all other communication stopped, waiting for Lady Reynolds' answer.

That lady did not disappoint. "I believe my granddaughter is more than capable of becoming a duchess if she finds the man acceptable. I will not sit here while you insinuate, no, while you tell me, that she is not. I believe your carriage has drawn up front for you by now. I will have my butler show you the way."

Then she turned away from the woman leaving that fine lady looking like a mackerel out of water, gaping at the set-down she had received from her hostess.

Daisy watched as many others in the crowded room took glee at the rebuke and she made note of how the other ladies took the confrontation. However, Lady Reynolds didn't seem upset in the slightest and spoke politely to two other women sitting opposite her.

Lady Gannon gathered her things and her daughter and huffed out of the room, but no one seemed to miss her presence. At least not at the present time and Daisy relaxed as she felt her grandmother take charge of the room again without showing any sign of distress.

Her grandmother did not say anything after their visitors left. Daisy was sure that the altercation would be the talk of other parlors that afternoon as word spread. But Daisy only felt pride at how her grandmother stood-up for her even if that lady was mistaken in her opinion that Daisy could be a duchess or even a marchioness, if she so desired.

Lady Reynolds affirmed that the choice for such a title would be dependent on Daisy's approval of the man himself rather than the chance of such an offer ever occurring being between nil and none.

As Daisy dressed the next evening for the Earl of Pembroke's musical, she worried her grandmother might suffer for her forthright treatment of their guest the previous afternoon. After all, Alice and James would not be present at the musical, having been ordered to attend a birthday party for an elderly uncle being held in Bath.

Their entire family was traveling for the event and therefore, Daisy would be without her staunchest supporters.

However, a musical was a tame gathering. Daisy relaxed, after greeting their host and hostess. Once she was sure no one was going to attack her grandmother for her outspokenness, she allowed the older woman to move about the room speaking to friends.

Daisy was also mistaken when she assumed that the evening would be a minor event. The room was filled almost past capacity, the doors leading to the balconies closed due to the unseasonably cold evening, giving no respite from the crowd.

Daisy began to feel the eyes of everyone upon her, the speculation again rife as Lady Gannon made her appearance at the Pembroke home. Her daughter practically hung on the arm of her recently affianced, Baron Sutton, a pimple faced young man in need of a toothbrush.

It seemed the recent engagement had given Lady Gannon a sense of strength from which to launch an attack and she cornered Lady Reynolds at the refreshment table. There, she proceeded to berate the older lady for her granddaughter's lack of prominence as well as lack of prospects.

Daisy had never seen her grandmother as she must have looked as a young woman but she thought the woman now facing Lady Gannon came close. Gone was the frail appearing, elderly woman and in her place, was a woman who stood as if her back were made of steel.

She gave Lady Gannon a glare that would have withered anyone of more sense and said, "Madam, if my granddaughter had a mother as stupid and as boorish as your daughter has, I would be content with her choosing the first young pup to make an offer for her, also."

The crowd surrounding the table and taking in the tableau in front of them sniggered and some turned away so that Lady Gannon didn't add them to her gun-sights.

Lady Reynolds set her glass of punch down on the table and turned, seeking Daisy's gaze as she did to indicate they should leave. They told their hosts farewell and, wearing their summer shawls, waited for their carriage to be brought around. The sounds from the other guests hushed and was just retuning to a normal level as Daisy and her grandmother stepped onto the stoop to enter their conveyance.

The next day was an at home day for Lady Reynolds and although Daisy tried to talk her grandmother out of accepting visitors, the older lady said she refused to be bullied by a trumped-up mushroom like Lady Gannon. Once again, it seemed like the parlor of Lady Reynolds was the place to find all the juicy bits of scandal that might materialize on an otherwise quiet and sedate afternoon.

The kitchen became used to the additional mouths to feed so by this time took the deluge of interested guests with aplomb and no one waited for additional refreshments at any time.

Daisy was on pins and needles at first, worried about any possible backlash for her usually gentle grandmother, but most visitors seemed to be there to show support if not to get the whole story.

Lady Reynolds held court, but did not bring up the unpleasantness of the evening before nor would she ever. As she had taught Daisy, she had said her piece to the person concerned and a lady did not need to justify herself after that. Those who came to get a few more salacious quotes or reasons for the contretemps in the first place, left full of pleasant foods and empty of anything on which to entertain their dinner companions that evening.

They did not have an activity scheduled for that evening for which Daisy was thankful. She knew the afternoon visit had taken a lot of strength for her grandmother to sit through and act the refined lady she was. Daisy wanted to tell all the women who were there to leave if they only wanted more scandal. That her grandmother was more well-bred than to speak behind someone's back. The occurrence of the night before should have proven that already.

Daisy sent her grandmother up to rest while she went to gather the notes and poems from the gifts sent that morning and placed them in the morning room. Sending the thank you notes for such items was getting a bit tedious, especially how to tell a young man that although the thought of him loving her from afar may seem romantic, at times it simply made him sound a bit creepy. Like he was spying on her from across the park or thinking of her dressed less than fully.

Daisy was entering yet another ball searching for her usual group of friends since Alice and James had returned to town. When she saw the tall figure of a man, his head bent to listen to a matron speaking from behind a fan, her heart began beating in double time. Her hands, she knew, would have become sweaty if not for her gloves. She peered around for somewhere to hide out of the way, ignoring the beckoning palms in the corner in case those, too, were the domain of her nemesis from whom she was trying to hide.

Nowhere seemed safe and she hadn't a clue as to where the ladies' withdrawing room was located. Spotting the closed doors leading out to a balcony or garden, she discretely made her way over to them turning the handle to silently slide out and into the welcoming darkness. The darkness may have been welcoming, but the unusually cold evening air was not.

Daisy wrapped her arms around her body trying to protect her bare arms with her hands. She would not need to remain out there for the whole evening. Lord Ashton rarely stayed very long at these things and if he didn't see her, he may simply leave without asking for another dance. After all, he hadn't sent a note this time asking to be placed on her dance card. At this point, the entire card was empty.

A shaft of light announced another visitor to the balcony and Daisy pushed herself up into the trellis of leafy green, trying to once again make herself less noticeable. Evidently, she should have chosen the palm since the outside balcony seemed to belong to the Marquess of Ashton.

"Come out of those bushes before you get some sort of poison rash or some such thing. I won't stay long. I merely wish to apologize to you if my attentions have brought you and your grandmother discomfort," he told the waif-like figure in front of him.

"You must have been misinformed, my lord. My grandmother and I are quite comfortable, at all times. The contretemps you may have heard of was but a trifle, the usual outcome when a confrontational matron challenges a lady. That lady often is forced to put the impolite matron in her place."

William felt his mouth turn up on the corners in humor at the wording of the set down. This young woman was going to be the death of him if he didn't stop allowing what she did and what happened to her to get under his skin. He tried a different approach.

"I must apologize again, then, for I thought my actions at the Dandales placed you in a position that brought undue attention. These matchmaking schemes among the ton are one reason I usually shun most events of the season, but I always feel I should put in an appearance with close friends and relatives. Otherwise, I stay close to my clubs."

"I accept your apology on Grandmother's behalf as well as for myself, although I do not hold you in any way to blame. There are only a few more weeks of the season and then I can return home and my parents can feel they performed their parental duties by me. My grandmother can return to living the quiet non-disruptive life she had been enjoying before I arrived and I can help my mother prepare for my new sibling."

"You would really return home? Do you not think after experiencing a season you might miss the excitement? The conversation? The entertainments and dancing?"

"I am glad that my parents forced me to have the season and I have enjoyed spending time with my maternal grandmother. But I will look forward to going home where I can speak without worrying how someone will misinterpret what I say or gossip about how loudly I laughed or how often I danced with the same man."

William smiled at his own arrogance and noticed when Daisy once again placed her hands on her bare arms.

"Here let me loan you my jacket to protect you from the chill air."

He quickly removed his coat and went to place it around her body. The music became louder when the balcony doors burst open followed by several young men laughing, the leader holding a stolen bottle of brandy in his hand. The raucous men came to an immediate stop and peered at the couple highlighted by the shaft of light coming through the still open door.

The young lord with the bottle found his senses first and stuttered, "Oh, s-s-sorry about that, my lord. I, ah, we were just looking for a secluded place to, er, to ah, well don't need the balcony as much as you do. We'll simply go back inside…."

The young men, light and music receded as the door snapped shut. William hung his head to his chest trying to think of the words he needed to keep Daisy from becoming hysterical at being found out here alone in the dark with him partially undressed.

The men who had withdrawn from the balcony would be distributing the tale even now. How they found the Marquess of Ashton, in his shirtsleeves, in the dark with an unmarried female. That was all it would need to spread around the party faster than a fire in dry grass, and Daisy's reputation would be in shreds. Damnation, he would need to offer for her.

"Do not say it, my lord," Daisy said bluntly, as she handed him his coat jacket and walked as a queen to the gallows, head held high and chin up, back into the ball.

Getting back into the ballroom was simple and no one had time to learn all the salacious bits and pieces yet so the way was clear for Daisy to walk over to her grandmother and say, "Grandmother, we must leave now. I have a headache coming on."

That lady looked up from her chair and answered worriedly, "Of course, my dear, we will retrieve our shawls and leave at once."

Inside their coach her grandmother asked, "Has this something to do with Lady Gannon again? Has someone approached you with more gossip?"

"No, this time I brought it upon my own head and I had to get you out of there before it became well-known by all those attending. I am sorry for what I know is to follow. I will take myself home as soon as I can make the arrangements."

Daisy was sorry beyond words for the scandal and embarrassment her grandmother would have to face even after Daisy returned to the country.

"You are frightening me, dearest. What could you have said or done that would put you so beyond the pale?" The older woman's voice wavered with concern.

"I will tell you everything as soon as we reach home, I promise. It is not really so bad. I mean no one is maimed or actually damaged in any way. Only a few ton rules broken," Daisy confessed.

"Oh, those. Society's rules are often broken and sometimes trampled and everything comes right the next day. Saying my lady to a duchess or not going into a deep enough curtsy for a duke can be forgiven at an event such as we just attended. I am sure you have over-stated the misstep."

Daisy became quiet as they continued home. If only it had been as simple as any of those faux pas, but it was more than a simple etiquette slip. She had been outside with a half-clothed man. In the dark. Alone. Moreover, had been seen as well as recognized. Her season was over, her search for a husband was over, her life, as she knew it, was over. What was worse of all, was that her lovely, fiercely devoted grandmother would take all the blame upon herself for not being a proper companion to prevent all of it from happening.

CHAPTER FIVE

If Tuttle was surprised at their abrupt return, he didn't show it. Daisy and her grandmother ascended the stairs to their rooms and both allowed their maids to ready them for sleep. However, neither lady went to bed.

Daisy sent the downstairs maid acting as her lady's maid back to the kitchen. She knew there was too much to think over, yet, and sleep was hours away. Instead, Daisy went to her grandmother's room knowing that lady would be unable to close her eyes until she heard what Daisy had done that night.

"Grandmother, I wish you to know how much I appreciated everything you have done for me to give me my season. I enjoyed it more than I ever thought I would and it is all due to your guidance and perseverance under unusual circumstances. Mother can be proud of the strength and wisdom you guided me with. She could not have done it better."

"Daisy, my dear, you are frightening me. What possibly could have happened to have you speaking in this way, as if you were leaving...."

"I am leaving, or I will be as soon as I can make the arrangements to return home." Taking a deep breath, she continued, "I was trying to get some fresh air when Lord Ashton must have seen me leave through the balcony door. He followed me to apologize for anything he may have done to cause the problem with Lady Gannon. He apologized to both of us which I accepted."

"I do not see how that is a problem. Lord Ashton

certainly was not to blame for what that woman said about you. He may have been the cause of her jealousy, but not to blame."

"I know and that is why I accepted his apology readily, but we continued to talk and he thought I appeared cold. He removed his coat to place about my arms and that was when several young men who were already in their cups appeared."

"Oh, dear, and they saw you two. But did they recognize you both?" Lady Reynolds asked hopefully.

"I am afraid so," Daisy answered despondently.

"What did the marquess say?"

"What could he say?" Daisy searched her mind. "I think he was about to apologize once again, but I stopped him and left the balcony and went right in to you. I wanted to get you out of there before the entire ton knew of my poor judgment."

Daisy's grandmother gazed at her granddaughter but remained mute.

"I will leave as quickly as I can and then everything will calm down. In a few weeks, no one will even remember I was ever in London," Daisy said trying to sooth her grandmother's emotions.

"But do you not think that the marquess will make this, right? He might make an offer and all would be forgiven and forgotten and then…."

"No, Grandmother, no. I would not accept him on such a lame reason as that we were found on a balcony together. You know I am not marchioness material no matter how well you defended me against Lady Gannon's attack."

As Lady Reynolds attempted to argue, Daisy began to tuck that lady into her bed. "I do not wish you to worry about this anymore. I will leave with remembering only the good about our time together and you can return to your quiet life with your friends and your afternoon whist games. I love you, always remember that. I cherish the time we had together."

Daisy went back to her room but knew she wouldn't sleep. She went over and over the activities of the night before, regretting her actions for perhaps the first time in her entire life. If she hadn't panicked upon seeing the marquess in the ballroom, if she had simply sought out her friends instead of fleeing, if she had hidden behind the palm instead of the secluded balcony, if she had immediately returned inside when Lord Ashton found her. So many opportunities to change the outcome of the evening. And she had chosen the wrong one.

She thought about how her returning home early would affect her parents. They planned on having this time alone together before the birth of their second child. A time to be the couple they had grown accustomed to being once Daisy was old enough to be left on her own. All changed on a whim.

Remembering Lord Ashton standing on the balcony as she left him, his jacket in his hand and his head lowered in thought. It was blessedly too dark to see his features, to see the anger or regret on his face at being found with her. However, it did not matter what his emotions were. She was going to take charge of her life and she was leaving London.

Let the ton think what they liked. As long as it didn't affect her grandmother, as long as that lady didn't feel she need defend Daisy, then the scandal would subside and be replaced by yet another. Some other hapless debutante would take a misstep and replace Daisy in every ones' minds. Not that Daisy wished ill onto any other poor girl but she knew the ton's need for fresh blood.

As the dawn began to show in the east, Daisy got up and began getting ready for her day. She would make sure the butler knew that she and Lady Reynolds would not be at home today. They both needed time to assimilate their new positions and did not need the avid eyes of the ton watching their every move.

Daisy sensed rather than saw the missive setting on the salver as she went through the foyer to the morning room. Walking over, she found a note addressed to Lady Reynolds in a hand she knew, even though she had only seen it the once. Slipping the envelope into her hand, she left with it, to read in private, fearing what the man would tell her grandmother about their nighttime visit.

Taking only a pot of tea to break her fast, Daisy waited until she was alone to open the sealed envelope. She ran her eyes quickly down the neatly scripted lines of writing before returning to the top. *My Dear Lady Reynolds, I am petitioning for a meeting with you this afternoon at two of the clock to speak with you concerning the events of the past evening. I beg that you withhold any thought on the matter until we can converse in person. Your humble servant, William Ashton, Marquess of Ashton.*

Daisy dropped her hand to her side and noted the paper was trembling. She wasn't sure if it were with excitement that the man, she could not stop thinking about all night was to be here in a few hours, or if in fear that he was coming to do something chivalries and ruin both their lives.

At that moment, Lady Reynolds came down to the

morning room and asked, "I need to know exactly what went on last night, my dear. Not that I find fault with your actions, but I wish to be forewarned to defend you, as I might be called upon to do in the next few days. Thank the Lord, we are not due to attend anything during these next two days. It may give the ton time to calm down and find something of more interest to talk about."

She waved the footman away as she continued to walk toward her favorite chair and footstool. "I suppose it would be too much to ask that some debutante run off to Gretna Green with her dance master. Then you could have been found in complete dishabille' and your antics would still take second place."

"Grandmother," Daisy tried to be as conciliatory as she could when speaking with the elderly lady, not wishing to upset her any more than she already appeared. "I do not want this to become the scandal of the season, either. That is why I wish to return home quietly. To allow everyone who is at all interested in my personal life a respite and find something of more interest, as this becomes uninteresting history.

"As I tried to assure you last night, I have gotten more out of my experience of a London season than I ever thought I would. I have met interesting people and made friends whom I would not have known. I have seen the loveliest of homes and heard some of the premier opera singers and musicians…. It has been all so wonderful, Grandmother. I will truly treasure these months that I spent getting to know you."

Tears welled in the older lady's eyes as she said, "Oh, dearest granddaughter, I will cherish these past months as well. It was like having my dear sweet daughter with me again. Once she married your father, she never looked back. They were so perfect for each other, so attuned with one another. I felt superfluous in their company.

Daisy smiled in memory. "As did I. They form their own little world and although I knew they loved me, they knew they would have to let me go when I grew up and married. I think that may be why they cling to one another so very strongly. They cannot face the possibility that one of them would leave the other, too soon."

Nodding in agreement, Lady Reynolds said, "It can be like that. I learned to love your grandfather. Of course, I was always very fond of him and I knew he would be good to me and any children we had, but it was difficult when he passed. Now it seems as if I have lived an entire life without him and it saddens me. I do not know how difficult his passing would have been if he were the love of my life."

Realizing her grandmother was getting too morose, Daisy said more cheerfully, "I will find the man I was meant to be with as well, Grandmother. He probably won't have a title or big town home. I am more comfortable in the country and with a few close friends. I will probably find a squire or perhaps a vicar. A man who knows who and what he is and will care and love me for what I am. He is out there, I am sure. Do not worry I will end up alone, dearest one."

"I will not worry. Anyone can see your worth without me needing to point it out. Now I have a few letters to answer, but I think I will remain upstairs after this, today. My sleep was a bit disturbed last night worrying about your leaving me before the end of the season."

"It will take me some time to get my passage settled

so you will have me underfoot for a few more days. It is probably best to rest though, take a day or two to regain your balance. I will check on you about tea time to see if you would like company."

"That sounds like a good plan, my dear. Do not mope about the place either or the servants will begin to worry. I will look forward to having tea with you and then you can read my letters to make sure I didn't make any errors before I send them out."

The Marquess of Ashton tapped his hand on his bent knee in a show of anxiousness as he rode in his carriage to the home of Lady Reynolds and her granddaughter, Miss Vincent. He thought he probably should be thinking of that young lady in a less formal manner since he was offering for her hand in marriage. After being found with her last night alone and in the dark, he felt it was the only thing he could do. After all, it was his actions that brought about the scandal and this offer and subsequent marriage would put it all to rights.

Daisy wouldn't face any censure, no one would dare bring up the night in question once she was his marchioness. Lady Reynolds could take pride in the fact that her granddaughter 'took' her first season and captured a title as well. He smiled smugly to himself, feeling as if this was the right thing to do, the only gentlemanly thing to do. He and Daisy would rub along well together.

With the thought of rubbing along well with Daisy, he found he must change his leg position. Even in a rocking carriage, he had difficulty not thinking of her as his wife. How he would introduce her to lovemaking, how she would be as unfettered in bed as she was whenever they spoke. Fresh and young and eager for new things. If she ever got boring or his tastes became too jaded once he set up his nursery, then he would set up a mistress to keep him entertained. Daisy would stay in the country and take care of his children. She seemed to him to be the type to do what was expected of her.

She was spirited but biddable. Look how she folded with the slightest threat of scandal, how she protested injury to her family name. She was very protective of Lady Reynolds and that fact alone would probably have her excessively grateful for his stepping forward and making the offer.

If her father had been closer, William would have negotiated with him. Since Lady Reynolds is Daisy's guardian as well as the only close family member in town, he would begin making proper agreements with her and finalize them with Daisy's father later. He felt comfortable speaking with the lady, and he wasn't planning on a large settlement. He didn't want the money, he wanted Daisy.

At that last thought, William once more felt a stirring deep down in the pit of his body and possibly a tightening in his chest. He did want Daisy. He had woken from sleep several times clinging to his pillow like a lifeline. Then reviewed memories of dreams where he knew he and Daisy were in the forefront. He imagined her naked legs wrapped around his hips as he thrust into her, over and over until her cries of fulfillment echoed in the night.

This time he crossed his legs over one another, trying to impede the blood flow. He couldn't arrive at Lady Reynolds's house with an arousal, ready and trying to stand at attention. He would need to stop any thoughts of the personal nature until he was home alone that evening. On the other hand, perhaps a quick visit to the little house on Curzon Street where he knew he would be welcomed having visited it before, would be in order until he was wed.

His carriage pulled up outside the address he knew to be correct and descended telling his driver to wait nearby but that he didn't think he would be more than half an hour.

The butler opened the front door and William gave his name, "Lord Ashton, to see, Lady Reynolds. She should be expecting me."

"Certainly, my lord. Please follow me," the elderly butler intoned. He led the way and announced the marquess as he opened the door to a pretty parlor with chintz floral chairs and curtains. It took William's eyes a moment to acclimate to the bright sun streaming through the windows. He realized that the woman on the sofa facing him was Daisy and not her grandmother to whom he thought he would be speaking.

He turned looking behind him to find the door closed securely before turning back to Daisy.

"Do you think this wise, Miss Vincent? I mean, after last night shouldn't we perhaps, at least, appear to keep to the proprieties?"

Showing signs of humor rather than demure maidenly shyness, she answered, "After last night, what would be the use? I am certain we are being hung as sheep and all that, are we not? I have received several messages from my still close friends that we are the talk of the ton. Now we must figure how to get through the next few days before I return to the country. My parents will not be able to accompany me this time. I will travel alone and certain plans must be in place for me to do so."

A flush of anger came over William's normal gentlemanly demeanor. "You most certainly will not. A proper young lady never travels unescorted, let alone all the way to your home in Sussex. I will not stand for it."

As if unsure of what he said, Daisy tilted her head in question but continued, "I should be leaving the day after tomorrow or at the latest, the day after that. I can rent a coach and driver, but I have no companion who can make the trip with me. My maid remained at my father's estate and the one I use here is too young to be of any help. I would be assuring her there was no danger behind every corner not the other way around." Again, that smile of humor at her predicament crossed her face.

"Miss Vincent, I guess it would be acceptable my calling you, Daisy. I do not know why you keep going on about leaving town. I am here to speak with your grandmother, and it should be that person to which I am saying this. I am here to negotiate a marriage settlement since your father is unavailable. Is Lady Reynolds about?" He peered around as if she were to pop up from behind the sofa.

"I must confess, my lord, that I waylaid your note to my grandmother and took it upon myself to meet with you. I surmised that you may be going to do the gentlemanly thing and quixotically offer for my hand. But you see, I will willingly listen to your request and then dismiss it as unacceptable."

"You are turning me down? This is a legitimate offer of marriage, young lady. I do not make such lightly."

"I understand, my lord, and I find I must decline. Not only is your offer unnecessary, I believe you will find that the ton will forget you and I were ever seen alone on a balcony very swiftly. Once I am gone, any talk and speculation will die a languorous death. You sir, can go on and offer for one of the duke's daughters who have been on the books at Whites for weeks."

William finally felt the need to sit and narrowed his eyes at his once thought-of-intended.

"What would a well-bred lady such as yourself know of the book at White's and how do you know what that book holds?"

Daisy gazed at him face to face and said primly, "Well, my lord, I see you do not pretend not to know of its existence. I do not know the ladies' names or any other particulars, other than you have been indecisive between the three. I suggest you select one quickly. Then your name would no longer be linked with mine and you will be able to go on as you previously planned."

His eyes hard, his anger barely in check, he ground out between his teeth. "I did not say I agreed with anything to do with the bets made at Whites. I find it appalling to drag a lady's name into such doings. What does interest me is how you heard of such a bet and why you thought I would be part of such a thing?"

Daisy appeared contrite. "My lord, I am not proud of it, but I over-heard two ladies speaking of the bet while I was selecting ribbons with Alice, um, Lady Alice. I have not spread the rumor nor have I thought about finding out the names of the young ladies involved. It has nothing to do with me. I merely mentioned the matter since you seem to be accepting of the fact you are going to be married. I thought you naming your intended would take the ton's attention off you and I."

William thought about how lovely she was sitting there trying to look demure when he knew she was feeling anything but. He knew Daisy probably wanted to kick his arse for getting her embroiled in this whole thing. And for forcing her to leave town before the end of the season in shame.

"There are no duke's daughters waiting in the wings, as they say. On my part, there never was a list of potential brides for me. I never insinuated I was even in the market after being so many years out of it." He thought a moment. "I must confess that my attending so many more functions than I usually do and even waltzing with you, may have led people to assume I was beginning to mature and think about setting up my nursery. Therefore, in a manner, I am to blame for the betting going on at Whites."

Daisy waved a hand into the air as if swatting at a gnat. "The men at Whites sound like they would bet on anything. Too much money and too much time on their hands." She gazed at him sadly. "It would have been an excellent way of getting you out of the gossip columns. Well, the ones linking us together at least. Now I am not sure what will make the gossip mongers stop linking our names."

"Why do they need to? I was serious when I told you I was here to offer for your hand. Allow me to speak with Lady Reynolds and she and I can come to an agreement in no time, I'm sure." He was feeling more relaxed than he had all day. Surer that what he came here to do was the right thing for him and Daisy in more ways than he ever considered.

"Then I would have to turn you down, my lord. I do not think we would suit. I truly do not. I am a country mouse. I enjoyed my time in town, but I cannot see myself living this life month after month all year round.

I cannot see us living till we are old and cranky together."

Her expression was one of pity but he wasn't sure for whom. "I would bore you. You would anger me in a very short time, and I do not handle anger very well. I do not keep it hidden like a pot with a lid. I will let it all out, let it blow like a teakettle whistle. Everyone within counties would know of my discontent, I assure you."

William felt something coil inside him, his groin tightened, reminiscent of his thinking on the ride to this house when he fantasized about her screaming out her release.

"I almost look forward to such abandonment of your inhibitions. I think we will be very good together, Daisy."

"My lord, I am not incognizant of the honor you do me, but I must repeat that we simply will not suit. If I must be blunt then let us be so. You do not suit me. You are hardened by years of women chasing after you, seeking your attentions with a simpering look or a discreet key dropped in your hand."

She took a deep breath continuing, "I cannot, I will not accept anything less than the love I see between my father and mother. They are so simpatico, so much as one that he became sick in the mornings when my mother first became enceinte', before they even knew I was to have a sibling."

She watched his face and any inscrutable expression plastered on it, but continued to explain, "I want to be a wife loved like that or never be a wife at all. I am still hoping that a man, any man, be him vicar or farmer will make me feel like my father makes my mother feel. I want what they have, the forever kind of love, one that will make me weep when I think of it."

"I cannot say if your parents have such a love or not, but I doubt it. I cannot believe that a child knows how their parents truly feel, especially toward one another. My parents were very fond of one another, I would say even loved one another. When my father died, my mother found another man for a husband and married again relatively quickly. I think they are as happy as my parents were. My father's mistress went on to another protector, although she had been left well off in the will."

"That is exactly what I mean, my lord. You speak of your mother eagerly remarrying in the same breath that you mention a mistress equally eager to change benefactors. I speak of love, a love that would have one wishing to die if the other did."

Now it was William's turn to give a wave of his hand as if what she spoke of was poppycock.

Daisy spoke slowly, as if speaking to one without full capacity. "Let me explain it this way. I love syllabub, lemon syllabub to be precise. Anyway, I love it and I may, if I like someone really well, let them have a spoonful of my syllabub. However, I would never, not ever, let even my very best friend take a bite of my syllabub off my spoon. That spoon and my syllabub are precious to me, for my enjoyment and I enjoy both in tandem. My spoon and I have an intimate relationship in that it enters my body."

She looked closely at her companion saying, "My life is like the syllabub. I may share it with others but the spoon is my love. That I hold precious and will not allow others to come anywhere near it, deprive me of it, or effect how it touches my life. I do not think you know what love really is, not the just-between-two-people kind of love."

"The kind of love you say your parents have and the kind you seem to be searching for, I do not think exists. I do think two people can blend their lives together and be happy for very long periods, perhaps even a few years."

"I want more than years. I want a lifetime or none at all. I think if I keep searching, if I am allowed to find my own way, I will find the man who is my soul mate. A man who understands he will never want to share his spoon with anyone but me," she told him. "I know deep down you are not that man, could never be that man. It simply isn't part of you to be so desperately in love that another person mattered more to you than you did to yourself.

"I would stay faithful to my vows to protect and cherish you. I should not have to explain myself to you and that is why these things are usually handled by the men in the family, but I was willing to speak with your grandmother. I feel as if she would understand the importance of my offer and of your acceptance. I fear you do not know how uncomfortable the spiteful scandalmongers can be. They are relentless and there are a few tabbies who have already tried to sink their claws into you."

"I was sent an article from the social section if that is what you are referring to. A Lady G was most audible in her prediction that I would come up lacking in the comportment of a proper lady. I only pray that Grandmother never sees that in print. It would hurt her so badly I could slap the smirk off 'Lady G's' face." Daisy held nothing back of the anger she felt at any one who would hurt her elderly grandmother.

"Nothing would show 'Lady G' and the tabloids just

how much of a lady you could be than to become my affianced. We could be married by the end of the season. Think about what a coup that would be for both you and Lady Reynolds." William dangled the prize in front of her.

"You, my lord, do not fight fairly. Although I would do almost anything to protect my grandmother, I will not sentence us both to a life of misery and eventual heartache. Again, I acknowledge that your offer has been more than generous, but I cannot accept. I will leave, people will forget, and Grandmother will return to her quiet life of friends and cards."

"Nothing I can say or do to convince you to change your mind?" He needed to try at least once more.

Shaking her head with a smile and rising from the sofa, she curtsied explaining, "It is devotion or nothing."

"I am sorry I was unable to converse with Lady Reynolds. I am sure she and I would have been able to convince you to forget your foolish thoughts. I will do what I can to keep the talk limited, but some members of the ton simply want to create chaos no matter what."

He bowed and left, not saying anything to the butler who was hovering outside the closed door.

Climbing into his carriage, he slammed the door in frustration. He noted a wide-eyed woman walking with her maid that he damned to hell. He realized she recognized him and the fact that he was leaving the home of Lady Reynolds, guardian of the Honorable Miss Vincent whom he had compromised the prior evening.

When Lady Reynolds woke from her nap and came down for tea, she seemed slightly disoriented and asked the same question several times causing Daisy worry that the older lady was more than simply tired. After having her tea and a frosted cake, the woman seemed to be as sprightly as ever, talking as if nothing untoward happened at the previous evening's entertainment. Or that society thought of her granddaughter as a ruined woman. Or that Daisy planned to leave London.

The next day, other than a note from Alice begging to be allowed to visit, there were no posies or odes delivered. Daisy was not surprised. Not only was she considered a fallen woman and not respectable enough to be seen in the company of properly brought up young ladies, she was now considered the property of the Marquess of Ashton.

The young gentlemen who didn't wish to find themselves opposite that man's ire quit themselves of her acquaintance. If she became the Marquess' wife, then that would be another story. Then they would write sonnets to her beauty that they would lament never being able to touch since she was a married woman.

All part of the way the ton lived. Ridiculous, Daisy thought. Why would a married woman want other men to write about her attributes, no matter how lovely? She should be more concerned with how her husband saw her, how much he loved and honored her. She knew her mother never doubted her husband's love and faithfulness and her father never doubted his wife's. That is what Daisy wanted in her marriage or she would remain a spinster.

Lady Travers, one of Lady Reynolds's bosom friends, was holding her annual pianoforte concert where some of the leading musicians could be heard throughout the evening. Lady Reynolds was not about to miss her best friend's musical and she was not about to allow Daisy to remain at home as if she were guilty of what people assumed about her.

Daisy and her grandmother were able to pretend they didn't see the ladies step out of their path, acting as if they had not seen the two women approaching. Not a full-blown shun, but close enough. Daisy thought the ton may not wish to offend the marquess and since society was unsure of his intentions, they were unsure of how they should behave towards her and her grandmother.

Daisy was trying to remain out of the attendees' notice by remaining in her seat even during intermission and forgoing refreshments when that break came in the presentation. She feigned studying the listed performers who still were left to play when she saw Lord Ashton across the room, standing and conversing with her grandmother. He seemed to be very congenial and smiling and nodding with Lady Reynolds and the conversation was being watched by many more people than only Daisy. Of course, such a meeting would garner interest and many heads were turning from her to the couple speaking across the room and back again. She could smell the speculation.

Gritting her teeth, she wanted to go over and tell the marquess to stop petitioning her grandmother because she knew that was what he was doing. He was possibly even making an appointment to speak with Lady Reynolds privately in her home. Convince her that Daisy would be better protected by marrying him.

Why was he bothering to do so? He could get any unmarried lady of the ton to wed him. Why make Daisy's life so difficult? Merely because she hadn't shown the appropriate amount of awe when he first spoke with her?

Was he that arrogant that she piqued his interest simply by telling him she would rather remain unmarried and return home than marry him? He didn't seem that petty. After all he was a marquess, what in the world could her opinion of him matter one way or the other?

The tone went off to indicate that the audience should take their seats so that the last performers could be presented. Lady Reynolds returned to her seat, but she didn't tell Daisy about speaking with Lord Ashton. The lights were dimmed and the two musicians took their place on the make-shift stage.

Pasting a pleasant smile on her face, Daisy stared at the performers as if they held her mesmerized. She didn't see Lord Ashton after the conversation with her grandmother and that lady feigned sleep on the short ride home.

CHAPTER SIX

Pacing in the morning salon, Daisy was fuming. She asked the butler to let her know if the marquess arrived to speak with Lady Reynolds and he told her he was instructed by his employer to do just the opposite. Daisy was hoping to intercede before Lord Ashton reached her grandmother. If he thought he could run over her personal beliefs and viewpoint, he had better alter his plans.

There was only two more days before everything would be in place for her trip home. She had even sent her parents her itinerary and was sure she would receive their blessing before she started out. Daisy would look back on her time in London with mixed feelings. Missing good friends like Alice and James, but gaining the freedom to say and think what she wanted without worrying about how it would affect her grandmother's reputation.

Daisy heard the butler in the long hall and peeked through the door as she cracked it open. She was just in time to see the doors close on the marquess as he was shown into the parlor. That must be where her grandmother was waiting for him. Daisy took a deep breath and headed toward the room.

A footman stepped out from the shadows and apprised her, "Miss Vincent, I am sorry to inform you, but I have been told not to allow you to interfere with Lady Reynolds' meeting."

"I really am sorry, too, since I will not be able to

accommodate that request. My life is being dissected and rearranged to others' preference and I must inform them I will decide for myself."

She pushed past the young man and entered the room that she saw Lord Ashton disappear into.

Daisy practically floated into the room, a wide smile in place as she cooed, "Lord Ashton, how nice of you to call. I am sorry but I must have been busy when the butler announced you. May I offer you refreshments?"

Lord Ashton narrowed his eyes to watch the competent actress in front of him as he replied, "I told, Lady Reynolds, I have just finished luncheon and so will do without anything further. The lady and I were about to hold a private conversation, so if you do not mind...."

"Oh, don't hesitate to continue on my account. I will merely sit here on the sofa and be as quiet as a mouse."

She plopped down and settled her skirts around her legs before looking to him to continue. She did not dare glance at her grandmother sitting in a chair nearby.

Lady Reynolds glanced from her granddaughter to Lord Ashton and back again. "Daisy, we will not need your input in this discussion, dear. Please allow me this privacy. Lord Ashton is a very important gentleman and has only a limited amount of time."

Daisy looked from her grandmother to Lord Ashton before saying tightly, "I will see myself out then, but please do remember I plan on leaving London in two days. I will be gone as I have planned." She curtsied to her grandmother and then a less deep one to the marquess and left, seething.

As she entered the foyer, she asked immediately for her cape and faced the rain as it drizzled from the sky. She planned to walk to the bookstore, about the only place she could think to go where she wouldn't find herself the center of ridicule or shunning. She would go to the book section set aside for antique first additions and other unfashionable tombs. No one Daisy knew would think to look for her in that portion of the shop.

As she sat in the park that Lady Reynolds' house shared with the others living on the cul de sac, she thought about continuing on to the bookstore. A burly footman showed up behind her, an open umbrella held over her head. The same footman who tried to stop her from entering the parlor and interrupt the meeting with Lord Ashton.

Daisy glanced up at him. "Is this your penance for not stopping me this morning? Now you must stand in the cold rain until I get rid of the sulks and come back home?"

The footman tried to keep a grin from showing. "I do not think it was meant as a punishment, Miss, but I have been put in charge of your care this afternoon. I think it is because there is no lady's maid at your disposal, yet."

"Yet? Why would I get a lady's maid just as I was returning home?"

The footman's neck turned red followed by a slow flush up his cheeks. "I, ah, I have no idea, Miss. I have no idea of the plans of my betters."

"I think the servants know much more than I do, evidently. Has my grandmother told the staff I am getting a maid? Has she told any of you I am leaving in two-day's time?"

"Miss, I have no knowledge of such information and no one would speak of our betters below stairs." He watched her reaction to his lies and seemed to relax when she let it pass.

"I sometimes wished I wasn't born above stairs. It seems like there is much more freedom for those who don't have to behave within certain restrictions."

"Except the freedom to speak freely, Miss."

"Go back to the warm house. I plan on walking to the bookstore and will return when I am less angry at the world."

One look at her damp companion and Daisy relented saying, "I see. You must really have gotten on the wrong side of someone if you must remain with me even when I try to send you away."

A stoic expression from the footman met her speech.

"All right. I will return home, but do not think it was because I need to do so. I merely hate to see you shiver one more time due to my bad temper." She smiled her apology.

A whispered, "Thank you, Miss," met her statement.

A deep male voice startled the couple. "I will take that umbrella. You may return to your station and I will accompany Miss Vincent to where ever she wishes to go. My coach is turning around now and will be back to us in a moment," Lord Ashton said with the regal expressions only dukes and marquess seemed able to pull off.

"My lord, I hardly think our being seen entering an enclosed carriage, even in the rain, would help put the wagging tongues to rest," Daisy said as she refused to rise from the bench even though she was wet and cold.

"Daisy, do not be foolish and catch your death out here. Please, come with me in my carriage or return to your grandmother's home. I plan on accompanying you either way."

"My lord, I do not understand your insistence to thwart my plans to return home to my parents. It cannot possibly be my declining your proposal has motivated you to conspire with a family member who has no legal right over me."

"I know you have complete control of your own life. Lady Reynolds told me and she also informed me it would need to be your decision, even if she held the power to order you to do otherwise. She is a very strong advocate for you, Daisy, although I believe she feels my offer is in your best interest."

"Then your business here is done. I am leaving London and never plan to enter society again, no matter who offers for my hand in the future. I find that I no longer care for any part of London's society. I have been soured against the whole ton."

"I am sorry if I have anything to do with your opinion. When I first found you hiding behind the palm, I was charmed with your freshness, your completely optimistic view of the world. I must say, it saddens me if now you feel London has let you down."

"I will survive the disappointment, my lord. After all, once I am gone, any tittle-tattle that is still being said about me will die and I will be forgotten before the end of the season." She welcomed the anonymity.

Lord Ashton, sitting next to her huddled under the umbrella asked, "So, do I have my driver take you up or are you going to return to your grandmother's house?"

"I may as well return to my grandmother's, my lord. I no longer feel like finding a book to read on the trip home. And I will return home. Thank you for holding the umbrella." Dismissing Lord Ashton from his escort, Daisy stood and walked back. Her heart felt heavy even though she had what she thought she wanted.

Daisy reached the door just as it opened for her and her gaze met that of the same footman who spent part of the wet afternoon in the park with her. Going upstairs, she changed out of her sodden dress and lay down on her bed. She ended up feeling very sleepy, needing to catch up with the rest she missed worrying about the clandestine meeting she knew Lord Ashton had made with her grandmother. Her last thought was to make sure she thanked her grandmother for standing up for Daisy's right to choose.

A loud rapping on her bedroom door had Daisy waking drowsily, trying to figure out what was occurring.

"Miss, oh Miss, please come quick. It's my lady, I, I think she's dying."

Daisy pushed her legs out through the tangled sheets and ran past the maid in the doorway and directly to her grandmother's room. There, in the hushed room, her grandmother's lady's maid hovered over the prone figure on the bed, stroking the pale hand and crooning softly.

"What is it? What has happened to my grandmother, Smithie?" When Daisy saw the pale face of her grandmother contorted in some sort of death mask her heart dropped and she went cold.

"Has the doctor been sent for? Has she been able to say anything?" Daisy, too, sank down near the edge of the bed trying to give some relief to the elderly woman she had become so close to these last few months.

"Grandmother, it's Daisy. Is there anything I can get you? Any way I can help? Please, please hold on, dearest, the doctor is on his way." She spoke tearfully trying to be brave for her grandmother's sake.

"I think she can hear us, Miss, but when she tries to speak nothing comes out. I found her that way when I came in to get things ready for the day like I always do." Smithie, her grandmother's long-time maid, wiped tears from her eyes as well.

Petting her hand, Daisy continued, not knowing what else to do to give comfort. "I will stay right here with you, dearest. We will do everything we can to help you. Are you in pain? Can you blink and let me know? Once for yes and two for no?"

Lady Reynolds blinked twice which led to Daisy's loss of control as she sobbed freely. Thankful that her grandmother understood the question, that she was not in pain and that her ability to communicate was still there. Hopefully a sign the older woman could also recover from this paralysis.

"Oh, dearest, that is good then." Turning her head Daisy said, "I think I hear the doctor. Grandmother, you should be feeling better soon."

A white-haired gentleman entered the room and without a word, went directly to his patient. Daisy and Smithie backed away from the bed, hovering closely in case they might be needed.

After a thorough examination, the doctor took Daisy into the hall. "Lady Reynolds has had an apoplectic seizure and the prognosis is not good. She may regain some use of her speech and movements, but those on her left side will be severely limited, probably for the rest of her life."

"But she will recover? I mean, she will be able to know who we are and speak to us of what she needs and wants?" Daisy asked him trying to be strong in case the answers were not what she wished to hear.

"No one can foresee these things. I have had older patients recover much of their physical strength and speech while others deteriorate at an alarming rate. Each patient seems to react to this condition in their own way," the doctor pronounced.

"This cannot be happening. I will not let this happen," Daisy whispered. "How can we help her now? Right now?"

The doctor thought a moment then sighed. "Have someone stay with her and see to her needs. Offer weak tea with sugar maybe broth later, but see how she does swallowing the tea first. As I told you, these things are different with each patient and her recovery may be very slow, if at all."

"Smithie and I will care for her. She will not be left alone again, that I can assure you. We will care for her as if she were her usual self and hope she regains more movement and speech. I hate not knowing if she is in pain," Daisy said worriedly.

"That is one thing about these seizures. There is little pain afterward or none worth the patient mentioning once they regain their speech. During the seizure is another thing, of course, but Lady Reynolds is through that part. As long as she doesn't have any more, she should be comfortable."

"She could have another seizure? One like this one?" Daisy asked not wanting to believe what the doctor said.

"It has been known. Sometimes they survive multiple seizures and other times...."

"No, do not say it. I will stay by her side and make sure she has everything she needs and there is someone to help her with those things she cannot do on her own.

Hopefully she will be one of your patients who make a full recovery."

The kind doctor nodded then left.

Daisy took charge of her grandmother's supervision. "Smithie, we will take care of my lady and she must never be left alone, not even for a moment. You and I will take turns. I will help this morning and then one of us should rest in the afternoon so that we can be refreshed to care for Lady Reynolds through the night."

"Yes, Miss, I will do that willingly. My lady has always been so good to me. I owe her for the years she has kept me on even though I cannot do as much as I once could." Smithie sniffed and wiped her eyes.

"Now, no more of that Smithie, we have a job to do. We need to get my lady back and speaking again," Daisy said as she decided to order the tea as the doctor suggested and to clean her grandmother up after the rigors of the seizure.

The sun coming through the open curtains shone brightly on the crisply white bedcover. Daisy walked over to the bed smiling. "That book I told you about has arrived. I know you will find it as entertaining as I did. I will begin it right have a little luncheon. Will that suit you?"

Lady Reynolds, her face sagging on one side distorting the beauty that once had been hers, watched studiously. She blinked once.

Daisy poured some clear broth into a baby feeder and lifted it carefully to her grandmother's lips as she continued to speak, "I also received a letter from mother and I will read that first. I have not read it yet myself since I wanted to share it with you. Perhaps we could compose an answer to her before I begin the novel."

Another blink. The only form of communication between the two so far, but Daisy was heartened at the fact the elderly lady knew what was going on around her. As well as recognizing Daisy, Smithie, the doctor, and the little housemaid who acted as Daisy's dresser. No one else had been allowed to visit since Lady Reynolds' infirmity.

Daisy was getting rid of the tray when the butler tapped on Lady Reynolds' open door and stood looking sternly. "I was told to always allow this gentleman access to Lady Reynolds so I am doing so. Lord Ashton, my lady, Miss."

The marquess strode into Lady Reynolds' boudoir as if he had done so many times before, moved to the bed, and bowed. He sat in the chair that Daisy had recently vacated next to the bed.

"My dear Lady Reynolds, I was sorry to hear of your indisposition and wished you not to worry. What we discussed is still an option. I still have high hopes for the favorable outcome as we resolved. Do not feel that this adversity has turned me away or altered any of our plans." He gazed into the old woman's eyes and smiled, letting his voice go soft. "Is there anything else that I can do to ease your mind?"

Lady Reynolds' blinked once.

Daisy came up behind him feeling justified in telling a lie. "That means, no. Smithie and I are taking care of her until she returns to her own robust health, my lord, but we both thank you for your visit. I must insist it be kept of short duration since Grandmother tires easily."

He stood abruptly. Daisy found he was standing too close for comfort and stepped back.

"I will have the butler see you out, my lord. Again, thank you for thinking of my grandmother at this time."

"May we talk, Daisy? Only for a moment. Possibly in the hall?" he asked looking closely at her face as he did so.

Daisy wanted to take him to task for using her given name, for visiting without asking first, for simply being too tall and too male.

Instead, she said pleasantly, "I am sorry, my lord, but I cannot leave my grandmother. I am sure we do not have any unfinished business between us even if I found myself unable to return home as I planned. I am sure society has gone on just as well without me in the interim."

Lord Ashton looked over to the bed and then bowed his head, "Of course. I should make an appointment next time. Tomorrow about three of the clock then?"

Daisy's mouth opened and shut, her mind whirling trying to find a reason to deny his request besides not having a chaperone. She could get a maid or even a footman to accompany her. However, since she had met with the man before without one, it seemed an obvious ploy to fend off any private time together.

Daisy took a surreptitious glance at her grandmother in bed clearly paying attention to the conversation. Daisy nodded with a brittle smile, "Certainly, tomorrow afternoon, my lord."

As Lord Ashton left, Daisy sat back down and taking out her mother's letter began to read the short missive. Afterwards she picked up the writing table and asked her grandmother as she was wont to do. "How should we begin the return letter? That the bright sun has made the room so much less dreary?"

Lady Reynolds tapped her right hand on the blanket in jerky motions.

Daisy noticed the movement and asked, "Do you wish to write a note yourself, Grandmother? Do you feel you can?"

At the elderly woman's emphatic hand movement, Daisy placed a pencil between her fingers and a book covered by a sheet of paper under it.

The old lady looked downward, watching the movement of her own hand as if it were performing a delicate surgery. The letters came out shaky and uneven but Daisy could read the words. She looked toward her grandmother's still paralyzed face and said questioningly, "'Marry him'. Is that what you wrote, dearest? 'Marry him'?"

One blink.

"You still think I should marry, Lord Ashton." A statement not a question this time.

One blink.

Daisy was flummoxed, and returned to writing her letter to her mother without trying to talk about Lord Ashton with her grandmother. Trying to block any thoughts of him from her mind, she finished the letter home and began reading the novel as she promised earlier in the day.

The next day, Daisy sat in the morning parlor waiting for Lord Ashton. She opened the folded sheet of paper she had removed from her sleeve and re-read the shaky message - marry him.

Lord Ashton was announced and as he came in, he pulled the door closed on the butler as that man stood uncertainly in the hall.

"I believe that we need the privacy to discuss what

is between us," he began before making his way to the sofa where she sat, the note quickly tucked once more into the sleeve of her gown.

"I am here only because you seem to think we have unfinished business, my lord. As you know, I do not. I did not wish to start a contretemps in front of my grandmother, but that does not mean I will not have you thrown out right now." Daisy raised her chin with her head high.

Lord Ashton sighed. "Daisy, you know your grandmother and I had a discussion. I told you she said she would leave the decisions of whether to accept my offer up to you…. She also said she would do all in her power to convince you to accept. We both wish only what is best for you. Returning to the country and watching your parents raise your sibling would not be in your best interest. And neither of us think that is what your parents wish for you, either."

"I can think for myself, thank you, my lord, and I find I am most comfortable in my parents' home. They would never make me feel unwelcome there." Daisy was having trouble keeping her tears under control at his unfair assessment of her parents' intent.

"I do not say these things to hurt you, Daisy. I do not wish you to be sad or to feel unwanted. But you told me yourself they made you feel insignificant, irrelevant. I am offering you a home of your own, a family, children to love and care for as well as being respected and taken care of."

"My lord, I am cognizant of the honor you do me…," she began.

"No, stop there," he said frustration plainly in his voice. "I only wish your grandmother could tell you herself. That this marriage between us was what she wished for you, what she thought best. I would not make that up if she hadn't told me so herself when we spoke of it."

"I know. She told me as well when you left yesterday," she said honestly, her voice soft and hesitant.

"She told you yester...does that mean she can speak now? That she will be getting better?" he asked almost jovially.

"No, I do not think she will ever speak again although she has tried in the past. She wrote it to me." Daisy took out the note once again and unfolded it, handing it to the eager hand he stuck out to receive it.

After reading the words, he said quietly, "Even after she spent her energy writing this, you still plan on turning me down?"

Daisy became silent gazing down at her hands now folded in her lap. "I thought I was doing the right thing. Leaving, I mean. Grandmother felt strongly against my doing that. Perhaps my insisting I leave rather than marry you brought on her seizure. Perhaps if I had been a better granddaughter, she would not be upstairs bedridden, unable to even speak to her closest friends and family."

Tears rolled down her cheeks as she thought about what all her obstinate behavior had brought on her elderly grandmother.

Lord Ashton moved to sit next to her on the sofa and put his arm around her shaking shoulders as she sobbed her contrition.

"Do not think that, Daisy. Lady Reynolds confided in me she was looking to get you settled because she knew she wasn't well. Not that a doctor told her of such, of course, but she said there had been little signs her health was failing and she was anxious to see you established."

"She never said anything to me. We didn't need to attend social functions. I didn't care about dancing or meeting so many new people. She could have continued with her friends and afternoons of whist and would now still be fine."

"No, Lady Reynolds also confided that this was the happiest spring she ever had. That having you in her home made her feel young again, like having your mother back during her first season."

"She told me much the same thing so I guess I did do something right if she was happy for a while." She looked up into his deep blue eyes and asked, "But what about now? How do I thank her for doing so much for me?"

He lifted the sheet of paper still in his hand. "She has already let you know."

The next day, Daisy, wearing a simple cream morning dress and Lord Ashton in his morning clothes, stood in front of a minister in Lady Reynolds' bedroom saying the solemn vows that would join them in wedded matrimony for the rest of their lives.

He had been with her when Daisy told her grandmother the evening before and that lady almost seemed to smile, at least one side of her mouth raised a little more than it had been. Now she seemed happy and content watching from her bed.

After the ceremony, Daisy went to sit beside her grandmother as her new husband took care of the paperwork and sent the Reverend White on his way with a vail and donation to the church.

"Grandmother, I hope you understand I wasn't

trying to be obstinate and kick at convention. I never meant for you to feel you were in any way at fault with the problems I encountered during the season. I understand the great honor I have been given by his lordship and I will make sure he has no need to complain."

Lord Ashton, walking up behind Daisy heard what she said but merely smiled at the older lady saying, "I am returning to my home and will be by for a visit tomorrow, my lady. I am leaving my bride in your care for as long as she is needed. I am content now that she is my marchioness and everything else will sort itself out in time."

He bent and kissed Lady Reynolds' hand and then Daisy's forehead, startling her.

"Oh, um-m-m, yes, my lord. We will look forward to your visit tomorrow," Daisy said but didn't rise to see him to the door.

Her grandmother having a distant look in her eyes lay quietly. Daisy felt a movement as the elderly lady patted her hand and touched the wedding band newly placed there. Then left her hand lying over Daisy's as she fell asleep.

In the morning, Lady Reynolds was dead. Daisy was there with her and one moment there was life in the old lady's eyes and then the next she took a little breath and as it was expelled, she was gone.

Daisy took the loss stoically and Lord Ashton was at her side within the half hour. The house and staff became solemn and Smithie came up with a suitable dress of black bombazine from Lady Reynolds' mourning wardrobe and altered it to fit Daisy. A black hat wreathed with black veil was procured also and

Daisy was dressed as a loving granddaughter ought to be.

Sitting with a cup of untouched tea in her hand, waiting for those friends wishing to make an appearance at the house, she said to her husband, "I know she wished to be buried next to my grandfather at the family mausoleum on the estate."

"Is the present baron in residence? I understood he was up at his family home in Scotland."

She didn't question how or why he had that information but instead nodded. "That would make the most sense because he was not a close male relative. He merely had the right bloodlines." When a thought struck her, she asked, "You do not think he would deny her request do you?"

"No, she is the dowager baroness after all and her place is in the family crypt. I will make all the arrangements. Do not worry about a thing. We should be able to travel even with the rain and be there in three days-time. Do you wish Smithie to come with you now? Take her on as your lady's maid?"

"No, I think grandmother made provisions in her will to pension her off as well as the butler and his wife, the housekeeper. In case you had not noticed, the staff here is a little on the geriatric side."

She allowed her lips to curl up on the corners knowing the staff would never have asked to be relieved of their duty while the baroness was alive. "The attorney is coming tomorrow morning to read the will. I expect everything is covered and then we can close up the house."

"Don't worry about a thing, my dear." As an addition, he said, "I had the announcement of our wedding placed in the paper this morning before I heard about your grandmother so we may have many more visitors than what we would have had to begin with. I sent word to my butler to send servants here to relieve those of your grandmother who wish to mourn in private. Food will be sent, also, since I fear there will be those who wish to see we are a couple as well as to give their condolences."

Daisy looked at the man beside her with less than delight saying, "Yes, knowing the ton as I do now, I am sure there will be gawkers as well as the sincerely saddened friends."

"Lady Reynolds was well known and well liked. Do not be cynical to those who are merely paying their respects. It is not what your grandmother would have wanted or expected from you," he admonished gently.

Lord Ashton was correct in that most of those visiting to pay their condolences were aged and deeply saddened by Lady Reynolds' passing. Many talked together in corners, reminiscing about youthful frolics and years gone past too quickly. Daisy was heartened by how many remembered not only her grandmother but her grandfather as well. A man Daisy never met.

Through it all, Lord Ashton stood by his wife's side, accepting sympathy as well as commiseration on her loss. Daisy couldn't fault him in anything he said or did. She thought she would feel resentful but she was numb, even when she thought about her marriage.

She wondered if she hadn't agreed to the wedding would her grandmother still be alive? Holding on to life until she knew her granddaughter was taken care of by the man Lady Reynolds thought would make a good match. Or would the lady still lie dead, placed in the silk lined coffin and set in the front parlor for all to witness?

Only in that case, Daisy would feel even worse. Feel that her continued refusal to marry the man her grandmother selected for her had brought about the death. Daisy was glad she could give her grandmother the peace of knowing Daisy was safely married and above the gossip and scandal of the ton.

CHAPTER SEVEN

The Marchioness of Ashton settled into the tufted padding and waited for her husband to take his seat next to her. "I hope the rain stops if only so the driver and roads can dry out a little. I feel sorry to make them go out in this." She peered out the window at the over-cast sky.

"I am paying them very well so we will not hear any complaints, I'm sure. It is time, my dear, for Lady Reynolds to go to her rest. The hearse will be leading the way and will probably make it to the estate prior to our arrival. Vickers, my valet, will remain with the heavier coach carrying our belongings in case it gets stuck in the mud or some other tragedy befalls it. He is very good in any situation."

"I wish my parents could meet us at the mausoleum for the internment. I know this is very upsetting for my mother, to miss her own mother's funeral," Daisy said with regret trying not to want the unattainable.

She hated to face this last time with her grandmother alone, without her parents at her side. She knew it was selfish of her and kept reminding herself she was a married woman now and well able to handle putting her grandmother to rest.

"You know your mother would have come if the doctor had allowed it, but your parents stayed in their own home during your season and you never thought poorly of them, then. Do not do so now. They will make the trip after Lady Vincent has the baby, I'm sure." He patted her hand consolingly.

"I know you are right. I worry about her health, too. Perhaps a woman her age shouldn't be having children."

"A natural outcome of the married state. You told me they were devoted to one another and that leads to…babies," he said chuckling at her embarrassment.

"I do not think my parents should be a topic for this drive. I will try to rest. It seems I have not slept more than an hour or two before thinking of something that needed my attention. Now it is all behind me. Either it is done or it will get done by someone else. The important duty, to bury my grandmother next to her husband is my priority."

"And taking care of my wife is mine, so I agree with you taking a rest. Here let me move you so you can lean against me and possibly buffer you from some of the rougher jostling. It will be a couple of hours at least before we make a stop."

The inn was expecting the marquess and his wife. Everything was readied, fresh sheets placed on the beds by Vickers and a private parlor set aside for their use that evening. A meal had been pre-ordered as well and Daisy felt quite cosseted by the time she went to her room on her husband's arm.

"Rest well tonight, my dear. I do not think the roads will be any smoother tomorrow. More ruts and boggy spots, I predict." He leaned down and placed a chaste kiss on her forehead before she turned and went into her room. One of the tavern owner's daughters acted as a lady's maid since Daisy didn't have enough time to find one to travel with her.

Vickers was waiting for Lord Ashton in his room,

but William sent him away with a silent wave. He sat and eyed the bottle of brandy his valet always left to help him sleep in a strange place and poured himself a healthy portion. Sitting back, he sipped the liquid as it warmed his throat all the way down to his stomach. This was not how he had pictured his honeymoon with Daisy. Not with his wife in mourning and worrying about her mother's health, especially with that worry caused by a late-in-life pregnancy.

How does one make love with a woman whose main concern is a pregnant mother? The death of her grandmother bringing all sorts of other worrisome thoughts to the forefront, including the possible demise of her own parents.

He found no answer to his questions, no easy way to bring his reticent wife to accept their marriage in reality as well as in fact. Not as they were taking the body of her grandparent to internment.

He had waited weeks before finally getting Daisy to agree to marry him and he could wait until Lady Reynolds was resting in peace before expecting his wife to allow him his conjugal rights. He was over two and thirty so waiting a few more days wouldn't cause undue hardship. He would need to push his natural urges out of the way and continue to hope Daisy would eventually turn to him for comfort.

He heard of such things before. In fact, he knew friends who swore attending a funeral was as sure a thing for getting tupped as attending a wedding. Both lucky for those men ready to take advantage of a woman in emotional upheaval. William had never tried anything so questionably ethical himself, but he wouldn't prevent himself from comforting Daisy if she showed the slightest predisposition to his doing so.

Perhaps he should have visited the house on Curzon Street. He thought about doing so a couple of times, but thoughts of Daisy always kept him occupied elsewhere. He couldn't stop dreaming of her under him, her legs wrapped over his, her moans of ecstasy echoing in his ears. He practically squirmed to keep from becoming visibly aroused.

How had he gotten into this predicament? How had a simple English miss brought a debonair man such as himself to such dire straits? Wishing all their duties were over and they could retire to his home estate where he could tutor his wife in the ways of lovemaking.

He finished his drink in one swallow, hoping it would help with his falling asleep without any more thoughts of his chaste wife sleeping right next door. It didn't.

The country home where Lady Reynolds spent the early years of her marriage as well as where Daisy's mother was born and raised came into view as the sun was setting. Her second cousin wasn't in residence, but had sent word she and the marquess were more than welcome to have use of the house for as long as they needed. It was a gracious gesture on her relative's part and she knew her husband sent a reply thanking him in advance.

The house was not as large as she would have thought. But then it was only a barony and large enough for a family who rarely had more than two progenies living to adulthood. The staff that was taking care of the house was more than accommodating and once again Daisy found herself in a strange room, in a strange house.

She could keep her tears at bay during the day, but once the door closed at night, she had a difficult time remaining composed. Dressing in her sleeping gown she sat with her knees brought up to her chest, looking out as the moonlight glistened off the mausoleum where tomorrow they would lay her grandmother to rest in peace.

She would probably never return to this house or visit her grandmother's resting place again. The estate belonged to a man she never met and probably never would. A distant male who won the rights to the land her direct ancestors had lived on for generations. Now she would be saying her last goodbyes and going to live on her husband's lands where she would be expected to be interred when her time came.

Shivering, not because she was thinking of macabre things such as burials and her own death, but for the total lack of physical warmth since her grandmother died. The closest to any human contact was sitting next to her husband in the jostling coach and the kiss on her forehead when he sent her in to bed alone. Not that she wanted anything more intimate, not with a man who was still basically a stranger even though they had been married for a week.

At this rate, she would be a virgin at her one-year anniversary. But would it bother her if that actually occurred? She felt some attraction to her husband, had ever since their tete-a-tete behind the palm tree. But could she see them as husband and wife? Be intimate with the man who was so much larger than she was, so much more sophisticated than she was, and so much more experienced than she was? She knew she was a country mouse and didn't feel comfortable being married to a marquess who led a life so different from her own.

The local vicar was amiable to holding a short service for the Dower Baroness at the request of a marquess. There would only be the marquess and Daisy as well as the household staff, some of whom remembered working for Lady Reynolds years ago. Now they were saying their farewells to the final member of the Reynolds line, the Scottish faction having a completely different family name.

Daisy was given a bouquet of late summer flowers which she left in the crypt alongside a book of prayers brought from home that her grandmother carried at her wedding all those years ago. Everything and everyone were where they were meant to be. Daisy felt she could tell her mother that both her parents now lay properly at rest side by side.

Lord Ashton and Daisy left the estate right after the internment. Daisy, for the first time in days, felt that her grandmother was finally at peace and had found her eternal resting place. She allowed herself to let the tears fall while her husband held her tightly to his side.

William damned his inability to comfort his wife. Knowing she was in pain, even pain that was inevitable, made him feel impotent. He had the right to comfort her, but not the appropriate relationship to do so. This was the first time he felt she wasn't holding herself back, stiffening at his touch while turning from him.

He held her as they rode nearer to his country estate, the home where he was born and where he hoped his children would be born. The children Daisy would give him if they ever consummated their marriage. That consummation becoming more of a reality the closer they got to his home.

Daisy finally subsided into hiccupping sobs and then blessedly fell asleep. She felt so slight in his arms, he was sure there used to be more of her. She still had curves, which he found ever fascinating, but she had defiantly lost weight since that first waltz.

He took a deep breath to calm and remind himself they would soon be at home, at peace to learn to live as husband and wife. Plenty of time to introduce her to love making which he was looking forward to the most.

Another night on the road would have to be endured before they reached his estate. William could wait that much longer before he became a husband in deed as well as in name. He would bed and remain with his wife, probably until she was with child before going back to London for a few months. He would return in time to be present for the birth and then back to London or possibly visiting some of his bachelor friends.

He leaned into the corner of the seat pulling Daisy with him, liking the feel of her warmth against his shoulder, her hand nestled trustingly against his chest. He was indecisive as to whether he wished his wife to get with child immediately. Freeing him to return to his life in London or if he wanted it to take a while so they could spend an extended honeymoon together. He seemed to lean toward the latter, being able to take time learning each other's bodies as well as what each of them liked.

For some reason, William was sure Daisy would be as enthusiastic about making love as she was with other things in her life. Coming to London for a season and living with practically an unknown relative showed she was adventurous. He also thought he could nurture her need for exploration and take her further into the life of sensual delights that the well-trained ladies of the ton never navigated. Daisy, he felt, would be amenable to his suggestions and expertise.

Not that he had too exotic of tastes, but he appreciated a bedmate that was receptive to more than a quick romp. He enjoyed the touch of a woman, the softness of a woman and the scent of a woman. Although it was rare, he found he liked a woman to take more initiative in the bedroom, show him what she enjoyed as he allowed her more access to his body. William was sure Daisy would and could be that woman with him.

Daisy woke to the sight of a large Elizabethan styled mansion at the end of a tree-lined drive, the chimneys showing curls of smoke in welcome on this chilly evening.

"Are we here, then? Are we at Ashton?" she asked groggily.

Her throat felt raw and she realized she must have cried during her sleep again. She hoped she would be able to stop. It must be so tiresome for Lord Ashton to have her wet his coat so often. She could hardly look at Vickers knowing he probably rued the day she met her husband.

"Yes, my dear. Finally, no more coach trips for us for a while. Our teeth and bones will need to become used to remaining calmly within our bodies. No matter how well-sprung one's equipage is, these back roads can be the devil." Lord Ashton grumbled about the trip now they no longer needed to travel again for a while.

As she sat up to stare out the window, she said, "It is very lovely. How do you ever leave it?"

"I enjoy it for a while, but I get tired of being alone with no other activities besides quiet, solitude ones and then I get on my horse and ride back to London and friends."

Daisy thought about what he told her. Did that mean they weren't going to be staying long? That they simply continued to his estate because they were more than half way there already? Or did he want to introduce her to the staff since they would have heard he married and bringing her here would be what was expected.

Daisy derived that although Lord Ashton said he did not care a fig what society thought of him, he showed a great amount of concern of how the ton viewed her and her relationship with the marquess. Peer pressure was more than a mere maxim for most of the top ten thousand. A narrow path that must be followed and adhered to, a way of life. After all, isn't that why she is married at this very moment?

The conveyance pulled up to the front-step and several footmen came out of the house, forming a line from the house to the coach as the step was lowered and the door opened. Daisy emerged first and she turned to wait for her husband, hoping she wasn't looking as rumpled as she felt. She wished to make a good impression and knew she appeared younger than she was although it had never mattered to her before now. Now she wanted to appear as mature and as capable as a…as a marchioness. Daisy wanted these people, more than any person in the ton, to feel she should have the position as their marchioness. That she would be worthy of their service and the resting place in the family crypt when the time came.

The butler stepped forward. "My lord, may the staff

extend their felicitations to you and welcome the marchioness to your home. We are honored at your presence."

Lord Ashton glanced into the house seeing what must be the entire staff lined-up and acknowledged his butler, "Higgins. The marchioness and I thank you for the reception and I know my lady is looking forward to learning about her new home. As we have been travelling all day, I am sure you would appreciate my lady is tired and will speak with you and the housekeeper tomorrow. For now, I think the marchioness is in need of her room."

"Of course, my lord," Higgins said while turning toward Daisy adding, "My lady," with another bow.

Daisy felt she needed to add some personal statement as well so smiling, said, "Thank you for the warm welcome. I am sure I will come to care for this house as much as it is evident you all do."

Each of the staff either bowed or curtsied as she walked past and into the foyer.

A short, rather round older woman curtsied saying, "I am Mrs. Higgins, the housekeeper, my lady. I will show you to your rooms, my lady, if that would be acceptable."

Gratefully pulling off her gloves, Daisy nodded. "That would be completely acceptable. It seems the ground is still moving under my feet, as if I have been riding in a coach for weeks instead of days."

If Mrs. Higgins thought this personal conversation was inappropriate, she didn't show it. Daisy realized there was a lot she didn't know about being a marchioness and now with her grandmother gone, had no one to show her.

The bedchamber Daisy was shown to was spacious

with several pieces of gilded French furniture, ornately carved and trimmed. The room itself was heavily plastered with extra moldings and ceiling medallions defining specific areas of the room. One over the large bed, one in front of the fireplace and sitting area, another above the dressing space. There were carpets for each of those areas as well.

Daisy wondered if only those designated activities were allowed in the areas and if there was some rule that the servants must inform on her if she violated those guidelines. She removed her hat as she closed her eyes, too tired to open them even though she had spent hours sleeping in the coach.

She startled when a female voice came from the dressing room and a young girl stepped out, saying, "I'm Molly, my lady. I've been asked to act as your lady's maid until you hire another. That is, unless I prove myself and then I can remain if'n you want." The maid performed a wobbly curtsy then stood with her hands folded in front of her.

Molly was young and pretty and eager. Daisy liked her right away but was cautious until she learned what her husband wanted. She didn't wish to make a mistake and needed guidance as to how to go on.

"Thank you, Molly, I could use your help tonight. It has been a long day."

"Yes, my lady. I took the liberty of ordering a hot bath since I knew you'd have been tossed about the inside of that carriage for hours. A good long soak should ease those sore muscles."

"Sounds lovely." Daisy agreed a long soak sounded like the perfect cure for her body aches and perhaps would act as a balm to her frazzled nerves as well.

She was eventually lying in bed, a fresh sleeping gown on and sheets that felt like silk and scented with verbena beneath her. She worried that Lord Ashton would choose this night to visit her for the first time as a husband and fell asleep expecting the sound of him entering her room at any moment.

Daisy woke to closed draperies and a banked fire. She found the bell cord and pulled it to call Molly who she hoped would know where she should go for food.

Molly entered in less than a minute, bright and chirpy, ready to do her job.

"My lady, I let you sleep as long as you wanted but if you desire me to wake you at a specific time or bring in your morning tea, I will do that instead. I thought with you being so tired yesterday, this would be best this morning."

"Letting me sleep was fine. It didn't take you much time to get here. I would have thought the kitchens further away, possibly even in one of the other wings."

"It is, my lady, and I know Mrs. Higgins has set time aside to show you the house whenever it is convenient for you. She's that proud of the place. Been here since she was a young girl. I was in my room up above, my lady, and the bell rings in both areas as does the valet's."

Daisy took this information and put it away in things she may need to know.

Disappearing into the dressing room, Molly returned with a day dress over her arm. "Will this be acceptable, my lady? I pressed a few others if you wanted a selection."

"No, that one will be fine. I am in mourning and one looks much like another. I won't stand on ceremony since I believe we are to be alone here."

She allowed Molly to help her dress and show her the way to get to the top of the stairs again. The hallways were as ornate as her sleeping chamber and she tried to estimate the age of the house, but failed. The outside had appeared so much older, possibly medieval with signs of a stone wall and probably a moat. She didn't have the experience with this age of architecture to come up with a correct answer.

A footman met her at the base of the stairs and offered to show her where the morning dining room was located. He proceeded to guide her through the state rooms and past numerous doors, some open showing sitting areas while others remained closed. Daisy wondered if she would ever conquer the maze that was now her home let alone find anything else within the warren.

The breakfast room was empty when she arrived but a footman appeared and took her request for a pot of tea and one soft-boiled egg with toasted bread. Daisy no longer felt like eating now that she was downstairs.

She wanted to find Lord Ashton but felt foolish asking for him as if he were a servant. Perhaps it would get easier with time. Perhaps there were certain rooms that he chose as his own just as she would probably select favorite rooms for herself. She certainly didn't plan on remaining in her bedchamber all day even if it were large enough never to feel crowded.

What did a marchioness do all day? If she were at home, she would have made menu plans for the week with the cook, then gone into the herb garden to care for that, followed by cutting flowers for the main rooms as well as her mother's bedroom.

She visited with several people in the little town near

her father's estate, often running into the minister and his wife, leaving or arriving at the cottages of those who were ill or aged.

She crocheted and knitted baby items for anyone expecting a blessed event, shawls for the elderly indigent as well as donating items to the church bazaar. When her fingers became tired, she read books she traded with the minister and books that came in the mails. She spoke with both parents several times a day, at meals and right before she went to bed. Over all, she kept busy.

However, was it the same for a marchioness? Did one expect to receive a hand-stitched blanket from the lady of the manor? Did a marchioness make soup and take it to a laying-in mother? These were the kind of questions her grandmother would have been able to answer without showing disappointment in Daisy for having to ask.

Lord Ashton, even though she warned him she wasn't equipped to be his wife, still would not expect to tell her every little thing that was expected of her. Besides, he probably had his own things to see to on the estate, probably as he was doing now. He was most apt to be with his steward or head groomsman or master of the hounds. Giggling with leftover fatigue, Daisy wondered if they even still had a master of the hounds. Again, a frivolous thought, how busy could a pack of dogs keep one man all day long?

Daisy would try to find her packed books and read until the housekeeper was free to show her the house. From what Daisy saw of it so far, it would take several days to see it completely. Perhaps she should take breadcrumbs in case she needed to drop them along the path to find her way back like the two children in the story she had read written by Grimm.

That was the last book she had read to her grandmother, just before.... Sadness washed over her and she left the table, no longer wishing to speak with anyone or take the long journey through this house she knew would never feel like her home.

Daisy returned to her room to find Molly emptying the trunks that Vickers protected the last two weeks. "Oh, Molly, that could have waited. I have enough things here and I will be in black for months, yet."

"Yes, my lady, but I was asked to find and ready your riding habit. I believe the master would like to show you the estate as well as the village in the morning. It isn't very large but it's got a bakery and a notions shop. I believe the local seamstress has been ordered in for this afternoon so you may select more gowns."

"I will need more, eventually, I suppose, although I do not plan on doing any entertaining. I prefer to live quietly," Daisy explained again wondering if she should be so forthright with the help. She never had her own lady's maid at home and only a downstairs maid turned dresser while staying with her grandmother. She would need to learn not to be so open with her speech with the servants, no matter how closely they worked with her. One more thing to learn.

Daisy finally saw Lord Ashton at dinner. After the gong rang and after a pleasant footman ushered her to the correct dining room, not the one where she had broken her fast. The marquess stood waiting for her and helped her be seated on his right taking his seat at the head of the table.

"I hope you had a quiet day today and rested. This may have been the last one for a while. Everyone I ran into while out with my steward invited us to dinner so we should be receiving invitations, mostly the local aristocracy that are in the country and the squire, of course. My parents always invited the vicar at least once a month so I suppose we should do so as well. He will expect it of us."

Daisy was stilted in her answer. "That sounds nice."

"I thought we could ride out tomorrow morning. I assumed you rode since you keep saying you are more content in the country. I have a couple of mounts that are used to ladies riding them so you shouldn't have a problem. Nothing too frisky. My mother and sisters rode them whenever we got together as a family."

"I did not realize you had sisters and I assumed your parents were both dead."

"Both my parents are deceased and I have one sister in Midlothian, Scotland and another in Northumbria. They married cousins and I can barely understand them now when they speak, they have taken to their new country so well." He looked up and said with humor, "Yes, I know Northumbria is English, but I do not think either sister knows it."

"So, my lord, it is just you now, um-m-m, I mean, us. Just the two of us," Daisy said nervously.

"For now."

Not knowing what to talk to him about and having the footmen waiting at the pantry door made Daisy's words stilted and too polite, unlike her more gregarious self. She felt strange. "My lord, this fish is very good. I suppose it is locally caught?"

"Yes, most everything we have here comes from the home farm or my forests. There are great amounts of game birds as well as roosts where we raise our own. The deer herds have been kept culled, but I haven't held a hunting party here since my mother died over five years ago. I used to try to get here twice a year, but it has been almost a year this time."

Daisy drew her brows down in thought. "The staff simply stays on, my lord, waiting for you to return, rather, in case you return?"

"It is much the same for all the large estates. After all, it is not uncommon for a marquess or even an earl to have more than one property. They cannot be at all of them all the time and most of them are entailed so must remain with the title. Our son will adjust his life the same as I have."

Daisy looked down at the next plate the footman sat in front of her. This was the second time Lord Ashton referred to having a family in the last fifteen minutes.

"I will get used to moving between the two homes I suppose, my lord. The trip to London was not all that arduous and we could normally drive it with only two nights of lay-over at inns."

Now it was Lord Ashton's turn to draw his brows down in concern. "Daisy, I planned on you staying here in the country when I return to London. Less disruption for the children and, of course, my town house is not equipped for a family. There is not even a nursery floor."

"I see, of course, we would not wish to disturb your town life. After all, you are used to your life style there and I am more comfortable in the country." Daisy became quiet and tried to finish her meal, but found she no longer wished to be at the table with this man, this stranger, any longer.

And she remembered why she had been so adamant about not marrying him in the first place. They had nothing in common and she hadn't been raised to live as an aristocrat's wife, putting her needs and wishes second to her husband's merely because he was the one born with a title and a....

"My lord, if you would please excuse me for the evening. I find I did not get enough rest today, after all. I will be ready for our ride in the morning. Simply let my maid know the time. She seemed to understand so much better than I, your wants today."

William took another sip from the rather ample glass of brandy, looking out the library window over the back gardens, a view he was not too familiar with since he rarely went into the library in this house. There was an office near the kitchen door the steward used but this room had been set aside for his mother's communications and, of course, a large selection of books.

Most of those were sadly out of date. He came here to find something he would be interested in reading that would put him to sleep. A sleep without the release he was looking toward his wife relieving. Now she had gone off to bed and since he was not dense, knew she had gone off angry.

He tried to figure out what he had said to make her upset with him. He certainly would have taken it back or at least apologized if only he knew what set her up in the boughs. He thought the dinner was going quite well. She complimented the meal, which seemed like a good start for the evening. She seemed interested in his family, another good sign that she cared about his being. Then? Then she seemed to have changed and became upset or even downright angry at being told about the home farm and the estate.

No, that couldn't have been what antagonized her. Daisy liked the country, she told him so repeatedly. He was hoping she was in a better mood for their ride. They may run into neighbors and he didn't want it said that his marchioness was less than happy to be married and in the country.

The horse Lord Ashton's groom saddled for her was a sweet mare, used to a sidesaddle, and not too fresh. She was also used to the type of terrain they would be going over so Daisy felt very comfortable on her after not having ridden since leaving her parents' estate.

Being a big man, Lord Ashton's horse was a couple of hands taller and being a stallion much more difficult to control although he quieted when the two horses were ridden side by side.

"I have Mercury exercised, of course, but he always wants to act up for the first couple of days. Trying to show me who is boss, showing his displeasure at being left behind when I leave," he said controlling the stallion as it side-stepped agitatedly.

"I understand not wanting to be left behind, my lord, especially when there would be no one left to be in partnership with, no one that was his master."

"Are we still speaking of Mercury or are we speaking of you. That you will be left here while I am in London?"

"I was merely advocating for the horse. It is a dumb animal and cannot speak for itself nor state its preference, my lord."

"Stop, saying 'my lord' in that manner. I am your husband and you should call me as such although I prefer, William. Even my acquaintances call me, Ashton."

"Certainly, if that is what you wish, my lo…William, although I have difficulty of thinking of you in that way," Daisy admitted.

"I like the way it sounds on your lips. After all, I believe I have called you, Daisy, right from the start. I have always thought of you as such." He looked over at her. "I am not sure why, but I felt close to you since meeting under the palm."

Daisy laughed. "That seems like eons ago. So much has happened and if you told me any of what was in my future at that time, I would have thought you a bedlamite."

"I am glad you can find humor in it, at least. I never thought for a moment that we were destined to marry. I only meant to show the ton they were being foolish shunning you for having parents who were devoted."

"I, too, am surprised every day when I wake up and find myself here, being addressed as 'my lady' and knowing I am expected to be the social leader in the district."

"Do you find the pressure of being my marchioness too troubling? Do you think it will be onerous living here?"

"No, but it will be a lonely existence. I will need to remain aloof, hold myself away from others and, as you know, that isn't truly my personality. I feel I must be on my guard at all times or possibly let you down, leave the marchioness I am representing open to ridicule," she explained, able to talk of such things out in the open air while not being able to even think of saying such things inside the manor.

"Daisy, you will not, could not do anything that would let me down or bring the Marchioness of Ashton ridicule. You are being too hard on yourself and making your title into more than it is. My mother wasn't from a titled family yet she made an excellent marchioness."

"I wish that she was still with us, then, my lord, because she would at least understand how daunting I find the prospect of being yours." She kicked her horse into a cantor and Mercury leaped to follow.

Hell, how did this get so turned upside down? William sat in Daisy's room watching her sleep. A fitful sleep by the looks of things but he didn't think she would accept him slipping into her bed to hold her close. Try to give her some of his strength as she fought whatever demons seemed to be chasing her tonight. He hoped it wasn't him.

She had left angry but more than that, she had left hurt and without much to look forward to. He would never be the kind of man her father was. So besotted of his wife he spent every moment in her pocket it seemed. The viscount never went down to London and had even forsaken attending his mother-by-marriage's funeral or to stand beside his daughter in her time of need. Instead, opting to remain with his wife.

Daisy hadn't said anything about that choice, accepting it as right, as proper, as things have always been done. She didn't realize other married couples didn't live like that. They were more apt to have separate friends, even attend separate functions if their tastes did not run the same. It did not mean the marriage was not solid or even the bond between the two people was not strong. He and Daisy could have a strong bond if she would give them a chance, if she could accept less than devotion.

He almost felt like getting up and having it out with her, this girl-woman who was his wife. She would have to listen to him here. She wouldn't be able to stomp away in a fit or hide from him until he got tired of waiting for her. He prevented himself from standing and walking over there, yanking the sheet off her bed, leaving her exposed to his eyes.

He knew she was wearing a modest gown. Knew it was thin and had a simple ribbon holding it closed at the neck. One pull and she would be naked in front of him. Then she would listen to him, she would have to pay attention to him. But he wasn't that kind of man. He didn't want to take her by force or frighten her into performing her wifely duties.

Besides, she had offered him his rights but it seemed as if their joining would be tainted. She would go through the motions, or rather allow him to go through the motions, while she gazed into the horizon thinking of England. Not the way he imagined their lovemaking going. Perhaps if he could convince her she meant a great deal to him? Could he convince her of something he did not feel?

He almost hoped she would wake up and find him there. What would she do? Scream? Cry and rant or lay there like some virgin sacrifice, tense and stoic. The latter, definitely the latter. William got up in frustration and just barely stopped himself from slamming the door between their rooms.

CHAPTER EIGHT

William was going to try once again to bring his marriage back to a position where he could feel he and his wife were going to make their relationship real. He was going to broach the subject head on and hope he wouldn't sound as if he were complaining they hadn't consummated their marriage. It had become more important than that. William was worried he and Daisy would never get back to the time when they liked one another, when they could talk as friends and not as a title to his wife.

"Daisy, I need to speak with you in my room before you retire this evening. I will send my valet away and you should do the same with your maid. I want us both to be free to speak our minds, we need to get this settled and we need to get on with our marriage."

"As you wish, my lo…William. I, too, think it is beyond time to settle this."

When they met, both tried to be open and conciliatory with one another.

William took the lead, wanting to get the basic problems handled, wanting to get his wife by his side and in his bed.

"Daisy, your grandmother and I agreed you needed to have the protection of my name once we were found on that balcony. I thought you realized the importance of such, as well."

"I recognized the fact my grandmother was distressed my name was linked with yours and that her society, her friends, felt I was ruined. I wished to return home. Some days that is still my sole desire."

"You cannot mean that. You said your parents were so involved with one another you felt as if you were an interloper. Soon they will have a young child to care for. How would you fit into the family then? Be reasonable, Daisy, think about your own marriage. What you owe me as your husband."

"My lord, since you are anxious to return to London before the end of the season, why not simply get right down to the work involved. Get me with child so you may be on your way and I will be doing what I must."

It was either contrariness or merely that he didn't like being told what to do, but William balked at his wife's orders. "We are not breeding stock. There usually is some sort of compatibility between the couple involved, the sharing of lives, and then the begetting of children."

"I think I was very honest with you, my lord. I told you what I needed in a marriage. I wanted personal consideration, love, devotion. I must settle with much less than that and I cannot see why you should think to get everything you wanted. I will bare you children, whenever and how many you beget unto me. Pretending anything else, I believe, will cause us both to become too jaded to be decent to one another. I will await your pleasure...."

Daisy left with her chin up and her head held high.

William threw his glass, smashing it into the fireplace, "Damn it to hell."

Where was the pleasant young lady he thought would make a malleable wife for him all those weeks ago? He was without options at this point. Would he be able to bed her and then leave? He did not wish to contemplate his lady wife's temper when he did return.

Once again, he sat in the chair near the banked fireplace watching his wife sleep. Once again, he felt the need to go to her to comfort what appeared to be nightmares disturbing her rest and making her eyes appear sunken and her skin wan.

William stood next to the bed and with a sigh, lay down next to his wife. Taking her body unresistingly into his arms, he calmed her restlessness.

She woke and tensed at first until she realized what he was doing, then relaxed and whispered, "What are we to do?"

"Remember we were friends first, wife, and now we are going to get back to that path. I like you and I think you liked me. We will begin with that," he assured her as he kissed her lips, knowing he was pushing his luck.

He felt her respond and found he wanted her to acknowledge him in a sensual way. He wanted to feel her body pressed into his, feel her lips against his, and her tongue wiping against his. He felt that he had made great strides as he felt her relax and begin to drift off.

"I did like you," was all she mumbled in return before falling asleep.

William was amazed at how much more relaxed he felt, too. He wanted to calm Daisy, to ease her restlessness when in fact that is what happened to him. He held her closely. Feeling protective and possessive, both sensations he had never felt before about a woman. In fact, had never felt that way about anything.

Other women were just that, other women. If they left his protection for another's he would move on to more accommodating sport. If he became bored with a woman he was seeing, he gave her a nice gift and often passed her name on to a friend who may be interested.

No woman had ever woken his need to have her for his own. No woman made him want to withhold her from others - other men who may find her as enchanting as he did.

He fell asleep lying next to Daisy, another something he never did. He never slept with any of his women. Never spent any time in bed that wasn't required by the lovemaking process no matter how late in the night it was.

William woke up alone and feeling lonely, unsure why that was so when he always slept alone. He went in search of his wandering bride. He could see the light shining into the darkened hall as he approached the kitchens. He could hear Daisy speaking with someone in hushed tones.

"I do not know how I feel, not really. I mean I am married now. A real married woman and it seems a little unreal although what we did was very, very, um-m-m, nice. I liked the way it made me feel inside."

Pushing the door open, he peered around to find the room empty except for Daisy standing at the stove, a pan in front of her. "Daisy, who are you speaking with?"

Daisy shyly glanced at the calico cat sitting at her feet looking hopefully up at the young woman as she cooked.

Smiling, William pulled out a wooden chair next to the table, pulling his banyan around himself securely, saying, "That smells good. Is there enough to share?"

"Of course, I was making scrambled eggs and

toasting some bread. Nursery fare, I'm afraid."

"One of my favorites and something my valet can make for me in the early hours of the morning when I come home a little worse for wear," he confided.

"Take these," she offered spooning the eggs onto a plate accompanied by the toast already spread with butter and proceeded to crack more eggs into the pan with long practice.

"So are you used to these night raids on the larder or is it due to my being in your bed," he asked as he forked a mouthful of warm egg watching her closely.

He wanted her, them, to become easy companions again. Begin to trust him to do what was best for her because, God help him, he found he wanted the best for her. Wanted her to look at him as she had when they were under that palm, when he took her into his arms for their first waltz, when she realized her grandmother may be dying and he was there supporting her. He wanted Daisy - not the sad distant woman who was his wife.

Daisy seemed to be choosing her words carefully. "I woke up and thought I needed time to think. I think best when I am doing something like knitting or cooking. I often found myself with the cook once I was too old for a governess since my parents so often spent time together. I actually can put together a passable meal or two, plus I know how to bake bread and pies."

"I cannot believe your parents were so out of tune with the world they did not know you spent time with the household staff."

"They knew and since I was happy, they didn't bother themselves any further. It isn't as if I was being mistreated. I was already a young woman out of the schoolroom. I enjoyed learning the kitchen and all that needs to be done there. I think it was a very good educational experience and one that any married lady should have as a background."

"So just in case I fall on hard times? You can cook for us?"

"I guess so. I mean here you are now, aren't you?"

"Touché, I see I need to be more awake before I take you on."

Daisy placed her portion of egg on a plate and took a bite, the need for quiet contemplation and conversation with her feline confidant both disturbed by the man in front of her. "I guess I am not as hungry as I thought."

She scraped the warm egg into the dish on the floor near the high fireplace used to roast the large pieces of meat for banquets and set the pan in the sink along with the now empty plates.

"We should get to bed before the staff gets up to see us in dishabille in the middle of the kitchen. What a scandal would ensue I am sure," Daisy said leading the way.

"Possibly, but you must remember that a marchioness can do just about anything in her own home without the staff remarking on it. And as long as you are doing it with your marquess, I can assure you no one would ever carry tales."

As they reached her doorway, Daisy stopped and almost put her hand out for him to shake, but instead smiled shyly. She curtsied instead. "Thank you for keeping me company, kind sir. I am sure I will be able to sleep now."

She turned, closed the door behind her, and looked at the large rumpled bed, remembering the uneasiness and restlessness that drove her from the bed an hour earlier. She found her husband too unsettling to remain with him after his kissing her. She knew he wanted more and hadn't come to a decision whether she could offer more when she fell asleep.

At least he was polite enough not to wake her when she had been impolite enough to fall asleep at his first attempt to make their marriage real. Had he meant to make their marriage real last night? It didn't seem as if there was more than comfort offered though she remembered accepting his advances. She thought she participated in them. She couldn't be sure. She had no experience to help her decide if her husband was in her bed for more.

How much enthusiasm was she supposed to show? How much curiosity? She was curious about the whole procedure and what she knew about the marriage bed was probably all wrong. It could not be full of pain or woman would have put a stop to it centuries ago. Moreover, it could not be very exciting or woman would never let their husbands out of the bed. So, that meant it must be somewhere in between but where exactly was that?

Her mother would have been honest with her, explain everything that would happen. But she hadn't left her mother's house to be married. No one thought Daisy's first season would bring about an offer and certainly not one from a marquess. If Daisy had found a young man she was interested in or one interested in her, then there would be a period where they would explore those thoughts. Time to learn about one another that wouldn't be complicated by gossip, and titles, and death.

Remembering her grandmother interrupted her thoughts. How could she worry about herself when she had so recently buried her grandmother? That wonderful woman had opened her house and her heart to Daisy the moment she had arrived in London.

Of course, she had known her grandmother, met her on several occasions. But that was just it. They were occasions so days were filled with holiday festivities or parties with no time to sit and converse with one another. Learn about one another. Not like the months they shared getting ready for the season.

Daisy was glad she had accepted her parent's offer for a season this year. If she had waited one more year, she would not have had the time with her grandmother, not understood her mother as well as she did now. After hearing about her mother as a young girl, how she loved art and music, how the young viscount stole her heart and hand with a whirlwind engagement, how much she loved being a young mother…. Daisy recognized herself. How she and her mother were more alike than different.

All the things Daisy learned about her grandmother and mother would have been lost to her if she had made a different decision last winter. Accepting the offer from Lady Reynolds to live with her in London was the best thing to happen. It was the catalyst for all the rest. Now she must decide what she could salvage from her other decision – to marry a marquess.

She knew William would leave her as soon as she got with child, to return to London and his life there. She would stay and raise the child, or children if he returned eventually to ensure a spare or an heir if the first were a girl. Nothing she did not expect when she accepted his offer. The offer her dying grandmother supported as well. Of course, her grandmother may have been excited for her because the man involved had a coveted title and wealth to go with it.

Daisy only wished she had had the opportunity to wait to marry a man who meant more to her or to whom she meant more. Hindsight was always so clear, but she wished to reassure her grandmother that she would be taken care of no matter how long it took the older lady to recover fully. That the marriage ensured Daisy would stay and care for her grandmother instead of being driven from town by the gossips.

That the marquess was willing to clear Daisy's reputation had been chivalrous, but she didn't think he would have considered Daisy if Lady Reynolds had not been so ill. That is when saving Daisy's name from ruin became so important to him.

Now she was a young woman living a life she never wanted, a married woman but not a wife.

Dinner had gone well, William thought. Now here he was sitting with his wife sipping brandy in their family parlor trying to take the chill off the day. Instead of lighting all the fireplaces for the few hours they would remain awake, he suggested they imbibe in the traditional warming of the body, by way of strong drink. Brandy seemed the most refined rather than the aged Scottish Whisky he preferred.

"This is very good, William. I like what the French can do with wine and a few extra years of storage," Daisy told him looking myopically through the liquid in her glass as if she could tell the future by doing so.

"Why don't you drink that one down and go up to your room? I think we have enough in us to keep warm now," he suggested.

"That sounds like a good idea, my lord. I will do

that." Daisy walked very precisely toward the stairs while William watched his wife allowing a slight chuckle to escape.

It may not have been gentlemanly of him but getting his wife foxed was just the beginning of what he planned so he could finally lay with her in the Biblical term. He had thought all afternoon as she busied herself with who knew what besides being with him. This was part of the plan to woo her into accepting their marriage so he could get on with his life.

Lately, his mind did not travel far from his need to have her under him, his seed sent deep into her womb, her arms and legs clinging to him like a limpet. He looked at the still half-full glass and set it on the table. He must stop drinking or he wouldn't be worth anything to his wife tonight. But first he needed to make a stop in the pantry before going up stairs to make the woman he married his wife.

"Wha... what are you doing with that?" Daisy asked worriedly. She watched William enter her room wearing only his banyan.

"I asked cook for a little favor. To make me some lemon syllabub." He carried a tray with one crystal glass filled with a creamy concoction and single spoon.

"My favorite, you remembered," she said in a sigh, stretching a hand out toward him.

Shaking his head, he sat the tray on the bedside table before crawling panther-like onto the bed reaching for the ribbon tying her nightgown together at the neck. He tugged gently as it fell open to his touch.

He whispered, "I wish us to become better and better friends. I want us to be husband and wife in all ways. I think it is time we become a truly married couple."

William slipped a spoonful of the tart, creamy lemony flavored treat into Daisy's mouth, which she opened like a baby bird as he lifted the spoon to her lips. He followed that with a kiss, a long leisurely, enquiring kiss. He tasted her, the syllabub, and the unique flavor of her lips.

She exhaled softly, "That was nice."

"I agree, that was very nice." He returned to kissing her lips, tasting her mouth, slipping his tongue in to swipe against hers, waiting and receiving a touch from hers in return, inflaming him with her innocent response.

"I cannot believe you remembered."

"I did and I understand your reasoning. I agree with your wanting to keep the 'spoon' for yourself. But you did say you would share your syllabub, did you not?"

Her eyes half closed, she nodded. "I did."

William took a swipe of the frothy cream and gazed on the pink tipped breast peeking out of the open neckline of her gown. He wiped the sweet cream on the waiting nipple and proceeded to lick it off, followed by sucking the now firm bud into his warm mouth.

Getting an appreciative moan from Daisy, he did the same with the other breast anointing it with syllabub and then licked clean by his tongue.

Daisy whispered in confusion, "I don't think I meant it this way, my sharing, I mean...."

William pulled the gown unresistingly over her head, stroking his hands over her torso and returning to her still glistening peaks, taking one of them into his mouth again. He finally took a moment to return to what they had been talking about.

"You eat your syllabub your way and I'll eat

mine...." He placed sweet whipped cream from his finger to her naval and once more sucked it into his mouth, leaving trailing kisses as he slipped down her body finally to find her most intimate place between her legs.

Daisy still warm and welcoming from the evening brandy as well as the intimate caresses, snuggled down into the mattress and allowed William more and more access to her body. She liked the way the cool syllabub felt on her too warm body. How it felt being licked off by the raspy feel of his tongue. She wanted to stretch like a well-fed cat, accept his mouth on her breasts as he made his way to other parts using the syllabub as a trail across her naked body.

There was a hesitation as he reached for more whipped cream and she smiled, thinking he will once more anoint the tips of her breasts that began to feel lonely and ache for his touch. How quickly she could become used to his attentions.

Instead, his next dollop of the coolness landed on the warmth between her legs and she jumped with the shock of it.

William lay on top of her legs, holding her entire body in place as he used his hands to reach her breasts and his tongue to seek entrance in the once private place. She tried to keep her legs together and move away, but he used his hands to spread her and lick as deeply as he could, forcing a whimper of pleading and compassion from her.

Continuing to administer his special form of concentration, her husband eased between her legs as she become pliant, like putty to be formed, as he needed.

She found herself completely opened to this man,

his hands, and his mouth. Sucking, licking, no area taboo, no part of her off limits. Just as Daisy thought he must be out of syllabub and would let her go, he inserted his finger and she bucked off the mattress in surprise.

Only low moans accompanied his movements, low eager moans that showed his pleasure linked directly with her answering ones as she accepted and joined his movements. Rocking gently, pushing into him she found a rhythm that brought her the welcoming ease from taught muscles and spiraling sensations.

William refused to budge, but now Daisy was pulling his head into her, closer so even if he wanted to leave her, he would be hard pressed to do so. Another growl of success, acknowledging his need to keep her close as she shattered into a million pieces before returning to earth and his embrace.

A chuckle escaped William has he climbed her body to lie alongside her as she tried catching her breath.

"I knew you and I would be good together. We were made for this. We were made for one another."

Daisy could not disagree. Whatever just happened was beyond anything she ever imagined occurring between a man and a woman. For her husband to do it to her or to facilitate it happening was something she would need to investigate further at another time when her mind wasn't still in a half-floating state.

"Spread your legs again for me. I need to be with you this next time," he whispered as she accommodated his large frame and felt the part of his body that she was too frightened to look at push into her. He withdrew and then pushed once again, penetrating her maidenhead. He covered her mouth to accept her cry of surprise and pain.

"That should be the only pain between us. From now

on you and I will enjoy our times together fully, I promise."

He tutored her in the dance of give and take, the need to fill and be filled, the need to find that release that hovers over a couple until they both tense, arch into one another and cleave to each other as spasms rush through them, anchored at the core of themselves.

Daisy was satiated, all feeling was numb, but at the same time heightened somehow. She felt parts of her body she never knew existed, deep inside, that still sort of hummed with life like a vibrating string on a harp. She curled into her husband as he wrapped his body around her. She soon fell into blissful asleep.

This time it was William who got out of bed, restless and unsure if what he did had been the right thing for Daisy. He had been worried she wasn't eating due to stress over their unconsummated marriage. That she felt he was rejecting her in some way. That he wasn't wanting to acknowledge their marriage when it was the furthest thing from the truth.

He had wanted her right from the beginning but due to her youth and innocence thought waiting until they were in their own home before consummation seemed like the proper path to follow. He wanted her to show him desire, passion. Perhaps that was too much for him to expect from an untried young lady.

Perhaps it had taken him longer than it should have but she had shown resistance to their formalizing the relationship, almost to the point that she ignored they had one. He needed to make her realize that their marriage was real and that she was his marchioness. Now he felt they could move forward from this point.

Picking up his banyan that he had flung off the end

of the bed, he shrugged into it. Instead of going to his room through the adjoining door, he sat in one of the chairs by the fireplace to watch his wife sleep. She looked young and still untouched although he knew better. He had thoroughly made love to her, not holding back on his expertise or the possibilities between a man and woman. Not all the possibilities but enough of them to be assured she would allow him a great amount of latitude in his bed activities with her.

She was a natural for sexuality. Accepting his ministrations while taking pleasure in them to the fullest and he was sure he pleasured her. He felt her muscles clamp down on him as she came, sending his own body into abandoned release. Possibly the strongest he ever felt before, but then it had been a while since he had been with any woman.

The next time he was with his wife he may not have such an earth-shaking reaction to her, although that would be a shame if he did not. He surely enjoyed his orgasm this evening and he would work toward repeating it if he could. After all, they had weeks together. Perhaps months before she got with child and he could return to London.

He expelled a deep sigh. Now why should the thought of him returning to London be met with less than eager anticipation? His clubs were there, his friends were there, and the work here was done for at least another year. In fact, he had spent more time here already than he had during the last three years all totaled. Why wasn't there more of a draw on him to return to town?

Daisy moved slightly, allowing her naked leg to escape the sheet. He wanted to go over and stroke that leg, slip it back under the sheet with his eager body following. That was unlike him, also. How often had he taken even the most talented courtesan twice in one evening? Not that he could not do so - simply that he had never wished to do so. Watching Daisy made parts of his body feel like they had been denied access to her body instead of just experiencing the most shattering climax of his life.

He stood and walked toward the bed, removing his robe as he went and slid in next to his wife, pulling the coverings over them both. He never slept with any woman through the night, never wanted to but this woman was his wife and therefore things were different with her. Of course, they were going to be different, he should have realized that from the beginning.

He would sleep with his wife but not take advantage of her in the morning. She might be too sore and possibly a little self-conscious and he should not place her in the position of being embarrassed with him.

William was kissing Daisy's breast before the birds chirped their morning songs to the sun. He could wait no longer to claim what had been his only a few hours earlier and even without the syllabub, he found her body luscious to his tongue and lips and woke her to even more passion.

This time he didn't need to depend on brandy or sleepiness as a barrier to her inhibitions. He felt her respond as he cupped her naked breasts and she arched toward him in welcome.

Daisy opened to him as a flower does the sunshine and this time, she not only knew what to expect but how to help them both achieve it. A quick study would be what William would have said if he had any mind left to think when she was done with him. He was certainly going to rethink not sleeping in the same bed with his wife. After all, what would it hurt to do so?

That night meant a change in how the couple interacted. After waking together and making love for what was the second or third time that night, William didn't take time to count, the couple separated to dress for the day.

William breakfasted with his wife and afterwards they rode out into their estate together.

After that first day, it became a sort of ritual. Sometimes including visiting farms, the steward needed the marquess' opinion on or to drop off a crocheted baby sweater for a newborn. The afternoons were spent in the library, both of them writing letters, working on the estate matters and reading to one another.

The evenings most often found them dueling out a chess game or a game of cards, keeping score of outrageous bets and wins, sometimes for William and sometimes for Daisy. They would then decide to call it a draw as long as the other would condescend to make love in any manner the winner declared.

William let Daisy win those games because he took joy in her innovative alternatives to what he thought of as normally boring marital sex. Although that was an oxymoron since their sex was anything but boring. He had thought Daisy was going to be a handful in bed, not a simpering miss, and he had been proven correct. She decided what she enjoyed and, better yet, what he enjoyed and wasn't shy about their coming together, often and fervently.

The problem was he felt Daisy was still underweight. She ate at most meals but William would wake to find her sobbing in her sleep and although he often woke her at the time, she would claim not to remember why she was crying.

William felt he must do something to relieve his wife of her melancholy.

"Daisy, according to the last letter from your parents your mother seems to be feeling fine so why don't we take a few days and visit them? We can assure them we will not need to be entertained by the neighbors or anything of that sort, merely a quiet family visit. You do not think that would be too taxing on your mother, do you?" he asked one evening as they were climbing the front stairs to Daisy's room.

"Are you sure we should leave the estate for that long? It would take what, two days both directions plus the days we would stay over."

"That is nothing and the roads should be good, at least right now since we haven't been having any rain to speak of," he told her reasonably.

"Let me write and ask. I think this would be a good time since it sounds like Mama is getting a little tired of being inside all the time. My father is probably so worried he won't even let her be driven to church. She wouldn't complain but I know she would like to see someone other than the few people who visit them now."

A few days later, Daisy waved the missive from her parents as she came from the foyer into the library. "Mama says we are more than welcome and she looks forward to meeting you. Father doesn't write anything this time but I am sure you will find something of interest to both of you."

"We can leave in the morning if that is acceptable," he offered knowing the sooner they were with her parents the sooner she would become the Daisy he knew she could be again.

"I will travel without Molly since my parent's home doesn't lend itself to a lot of servants. They will make room for your valet though. And I should probably tell you now that we will not be given separate rooms since Mama and Father have always shared a room and they will not think to ready two rooms for us."

"That will be fine. In case you haven't noticed, dear wife, I have slept with you for the past weeks and my valet gets to dress me when I finally return to my chambers. I do not live my life for my servants' convenience."

"I did take note of that fact, dear husband, which is why I was not too worried that it would affect our trip negatively. I simply wasn't sure how Vickers would respond to such treatment. Sometimes I find the man intimidating."

He knew Daisy was not used to a valet at all since her father did without one.

"I used to be, also, and then realized I was the one with the purse strings and the one he was supposed to be serving. Once I told him so, he got in line and we have been rubbing along quite well. To let out a secret, he says you are the best thing to happen to me since my school days. He approves of my sleeping with you even if it has thrown his schedule off somewhat."

Daisy got quiet and her cheeks became rosy. "Does he say things to you about our being together so often?"

"No, not even slightly. No valet would comment on anything so personal and expect to keep his job. I think he means I am keeping more regular hours, eating proper meals and am very, very happy over all."

He leaned over and kissed her, taking the letter from

her fingers and read the words himself to make sure he had all the facts.

"I guess that is all right, then. I never had many personal servants before and the ones we had were so busy doing more than one position, they never paid us too much attention. Even Cook, although I liked working in the kitchen with her the best," Daisy explained easily, back in good humor.

William realized his wife's appetite increased with merely the thought of the trip to visit her parents. He probably should have realized how much she missed them, especially after the passing of Lady Reynolds. These two people were the closest to her and, of course, she would wish to reconnect with them after such a tragedy and loss.

William hadn't thought of Daisy needing to see her parents because he hadn't been close to his. Being the only son and heir, he was treated differently. Sent away to school early, he hadn't even been part of his sisters' seasons since he was busy at school. It would have been different if he had been older. Then he would have been considered an asset as a beacon for other marriageable aged men to gather near his sisters.

Instead, they found and, as far as they say, fell in love with their Scotts. He was left in the dust in their hurry to live in the wilder parts of the land with those same men. Perhaps he would make a belated wedding trip and take Daisy north to visit them. He thought his being married formed a commitment to ensure the title, which his sisters would relate to. For some reason, he was more drawn to family matters since his marriage and his sisters and their happiness had been on his mind, recently.

Perhaps being responsible for Daisy made him realize he was now the head of the family. He had been since his father's passing, but it took marriage to make him fully aware of the fact. Prior to that, he thought of himself as a bachelor first and marquess second, if at all.

Setting up his nursery must have brought out more paternal feelings even toward his sisters although being married they were considered their husband's worries. Nevertheless, just in case, he should write them and make sure they know he was available for them if they ever felt a need.

The two-day trip went quickly even with Daisy excited to be seeing her childhood home as well as her parents again after so many months. She tried not to think about how much she had wished her parents had attended the internment of Lady Reynolds.

Daisy understood her father's worry. Travel for a woman in her mother's condition was always suspect, then to add in the age factor. Any travel would be considered dangerous to both the mother and the infant. Leaving such a wife when she could go into early confinement would have been impossible for him, as well.

Her father's home was outside a small village of Sumter on Whalen, the river meandering through the county and furnishing all the water needed for the farming and animal husbandry. She missed the place and the people. She had never meant not to return when she agreed to a London season.

Daisy saw her family home from the coach and tears welled in her eyes that she wiped away quickly. Not wishing her parents to see her tears and misunderstand their reason for being there. She didn't wish either parent to worry about her marriage. She wouldn't let them even think that all was not well with her life. She had done what she did to make her grandmother comfortable. If that were only for a few hours, then it was still worth it.

Daisy rushed through the door past the footman and found her parents together in the front parlor, her mother large with child and her father hovering protectively although protecting his wife from what was a mystery.

"My dearest darling," her mother said holding out her arms toward Daisy as she ran into the room, going down on her knees in front of her mother so they could clasp one another closely.

The older version of Daisy lamented, "I wished to be there to bury mother but there was no way we could even travel to get to you. I have missed you so much, my darling, but I am glad that your husband could be by your side."

Tears rolled down the cheeks of both women as they stayed closely together whispering and comforting one another.

Daisy said, wiping the tears from her mother's face. "William was a great help and made most of the arrangements…for everything actually. I wouldn't have known where to begin I was so upset. It was very quick and she did not seem to be in pain, at least."

"I am glad you found a man to depend on and who will love and care for you as your father has always done for me," her mother said quietly in return. "I will meet him properly after we have a little time to speak. I have missed so much in your life lately I feel we are growing apart."

"No, Mama, not ever that. I will always be here for

you and Father. Always your daughter," Daisy said sincerely.

Viscount Weatherly stepped forward and put out his hand saying, "You must be, Ashton. So glad you found the time to bring Daisy to us since Lady Weatherly was warned not to travel."

William accepted the other man's hand. "I thought it time I met my wife's family and eased her mind about Lady Weatherly's health and wellbeing. Daisy seemed to be fretting and since we were so close, I thought the extra trip would be worth her peace of mind."

Ushering with his arm toward the door, the viscount said, "Let us leave the ladies alone for a while so they may sort themselves out. We will have a more formal introduction to my wife when she is less upset and can focus on meeting you. She has been worrying about Daisy, also, but I was unable to come up with a solution. I owe you a debt of gratitude for bringing my daughter home."

"As I said, I knew Daisy has been most distraught at not being able to travel directly to you after the internment, but she was very tired. I wished her to rest at my country estate for a few days before commencing to another emotional reunion."

"We men have to think for our wives in most times, I find, or they would not be able to function well at all," Weatherly said. "Could I offer you a port or sherry? I do not have anything much stronger in the house, but I feel the need of something for a lift and tea will not do."

"A port would be appreciated, sir, if it isn't too much trouble."

"No, I have both right here in the library. I spend most of my time here and in the parlor with Lady

Weatherly," he confessed unabashedly.

William accepted the cut crystal glass and sipped, nodding approvingly. "This is very good. Daisy said that you and her mother were very committed to one another. She takes great pride in the fact, as she should. It is refreshing to see a married couple so dedicated."

As if selecting his words closely, Weatherly said, "I met Daisy's mother at the first dance of her first season. She was only seventeen and I fell in love with her immediately. It took me several weeks to convince her father of my true esteem and her mother even longer. Once those two hurdles were cleared, Annette and I spent every moment we could together until the end of the season when we were married. I never regretted my decision and I do not believe she ever regretted hers."

"A true love story and exactly as Daisy told me. It is truly inspirational, my lord." William felt he was gleaning information as well as insight into his father-in-law. Not that he believed most couples could have what the viscount and his wife had and evidently enjoyed. Such closeness wasn't for him but seemed to work for the man in front of him.

Laughing at himself, Weatherly continued, "I know how unfashionable we are, Ashton. My mother-by-marriage used to tell me to stop hovering as if I were afraid some large bird of prey would swoop down and grab Annette away, but there it is. I seem to have a constant worry that she will be taken from me. That I do not deserve the happiness she has brought me. That at some point, I must pay the penance for being so happy with her."

William chuckled at the vision Weatherly painted for him. "I do not see anything of the sort happening, so perhaps it is time you stop worrying unnecessarily."

"I thought I had. Up till a few months ago, that is." The viscount thought a moment before continuing, "As you can probably tell, Annette was not very old when Daisy was born. I thought I was going to lose them both that day. It was touch and go for a while and then I had a healthy daughter and my wife recovered without seemingly any problems. The scare made me more cautious, but eventually we came to realize there wouldn't be any other children and we accepted that fact.

"I may have accepted it too readily. I didn't wish to face the danger of losing my wife again in childbirth. It is a damnable outcome of a couple's love, the pain and possibility of death to so many causes. It makes one question what God was thinking when he designed us."

William remained quiet, knowing the man in front of him was voicing things left unsaid for too long. These words were certainly not something the viscount could say in front of his wife and if Daisy was correct, his father-by-marriage didn't speak with many other people. Certainly no one close enough to voice such personal feelings and worries.

Weatherly raised his head as if noticing the quiet and the fact he had spoken of such personal things to a stranger even if said stranger were part of his immediate family now. "I am sorry, my lord. I lost myself for a while. I guess all the emotion rising out of Daisy's visit home has made me contemplate things better left unsaid."

"I think, sir, that you needed to get those fears out into the open without your wife being within hearing range. I do not know the lady, but she resembles Daisy so much I think they must be similar in other ways, too.

Daisy showed a great amount of strength when dealing with her grandmother's illness and then death. She was stoic and strong when faced with taking that lady to the family crypt, in facing down the present baron of the estate if she had to do so. I assumed she would not be able to handle the situation, including the travel arrangements, but in truth she could have done it all alone." William admitted taking pride in his wife's strength.

Daisy's father looked directly at William. "I'm glad she didn't need to, though. She may not seem like she needs a man's shoulder to lean on, but I know she appreciated you being there just the same. And if you are lucky enough to have won her heart, as well as her hand, then you will benefit from her strength and love several times over."

William smiled and saluted the air with his glass before taking a drink in toast to his wife. He found he liked this man, the man who raised his wife and knew he would like Lady Weatherly as much. After all, they were each a part of Daisy and William found himself more and more attracted to his wife.

Watching the sheep from the library's window, he sipped his port thinking about his wife. On the two nights at inns along the way they shared a bed just as they had done at home and he slept better than he usually did while traveling. Of course, he also made love to his wife nightly which might have eased him into restful sleep, but he felt more refreshed as well as more, perhaps the word would be, 'content'.

Yes, William felt more content, more gratified than ever before. He knew what he wanted to be doing, where he should be and with whom. He hated to consider he was the type of man who liked being married but perhaps there was no more need for hiding from the truth. He enjoyed being married. He enjoyed sitting and talking with his wife. He enjoyed bedding that wife and bringing her enjoyment as well.

Mentally shaking himself, he realized he was thinking carnal thoughts in front of the father of the woman he was having those thoughts about. Not exactly unexpected since he was a newlywed, but one should not do so in front of one's wife's father. If there was not a rule of etiquette covering such things there certainly should be.

Daisy had been correct in assuming she and William would be put in the same room. What she had not expected was that room was to be the same one in which she had been raised. The same cream and sage green draperies and flowered bed cover. The same light sage green walls trimmed in cream woodwork with brass doorknobs. The bed, which always seemed so big was suddenly too small when compared to William's tall lean frame although it probably was a bed meant to hold two adults.

Daisy was putting on her earbobs when William reentered the room. He and Vickers finished earlier and both left to give Daisy her privacy to dress for dinner.

"You look lovely, as always. Have I told you that I like your parents very much? Well, at least your father since I have yet to converse with your mother, but I know you are alike so I should like her as well."

He stopped behind her as she watched him in the reflection of the mirror. He really was a beautiful man, muscular, masculine and so very, very good at making love. If only he believed in love, believed in two people who made one another complete. Believed she could be that person to him. But that was simply wishful thinking.

"I am sorry I became such a watering-pot upon our arrival. It was as if a dam simply let go as soon as I saw my mother. I cannot explain it any other way. A release of tension that I didn't know I was holding back. I should not have burdened her with it, I know, not in her condition."

Daisy looked into her husband's eyes in the mirror's reflection. "I simply saw my mama and everything I needed to tell her wanted out, about grandmother, about the wedding, about the failure of my season. I could not burden her with it all, either. They are not her problems to bear, they are mine."

"I think your memory is playing tricks on you if you think there is anything to apologize for or hide from that time. You became a toast of the season, securing invitations to parties where only the highest of the echelons are invited. You danced with one of the most sought-after bachelors of several seasons and then brought him up to scratch by marrying him. You cared for your ailing grandmother and honored her with everything you did before and following her death."

He leaned down almost to her shoulder still holding her gaze in the mirror. "Lady Reynolds told me during one of our talks about how proud she was of you, your beauty, but mostly, your intelligence. She repeatedly assured me you had a good head on your shoulders and would pass the ability to think on to future generations, my future generations."

She turned to face him. "Oh, William, I never knew she said all those things to you. I am so sorry if she put you in an uncomfortable position. I never knew she was so actively pursuing you on my account. She misunderstood why you were helping me, your making me comfortable among the ton."

"No, I think that very wise lady knew exactly why I was dancing with you and paying attention to you and keeping the other young men at bay. She was right to confront me because, otherwise, I may have let you escape home feeling like a failure when I actually held you in the highest esteem."

"William, you don't need to say these things to me. I feel much better and I will not say anything to Mama to make her feel that my season was anything less than perfect."

"It makes me sad to think that you have those memories of a less than perfect season. As I said, most ladies would have thought any season that ended in a marriage to a title, let alone marquess, would be considered perfect. Or are you trying to put me in my place?" he teased.

"No, I believe your place is where you are and my place is beside you. I do not know when I realized that, but it is true and I will remain there until you leave for London."

"London is a long way off and probably a long time off. We have much more to do before I can think of returning to town."

"That reminds me…how very, very maternal my mother is looking. I mean, I knew she was expecting my younger sibling, but seeing her, like this, makes it all become so real."

She knew she was gushing but couldn't stop the amazement from showing. "I actually felt my sibling kick at me. I felt the small foot push out and I tickled it and it pulled back quickly then pressed back into my hand again. As if it was playing with me. It is so real to me now and soon I could feel that same thing but from within me. I am truly awed by the prospect."

William, overcome by her words, leaned down and kissed her neck, placing his hand over her abdomen as if claiming that part of her body as his own.

"I cannot wait for that time. I look forward to your body changing and accommodating my child. In fact, thinking of such things before dinner cannot be good since now, I wish to skip the meal and go right to bed just as we both have gotten dressed."

Daisy raised her eyes to his once more. "My parents would probably bless our tardiness. I would die of embarrassment, as they would not need to guess at the reason for our delay. I mean Mama and Father missed a fair amount of meals which I now attribute to his helping her dress for dinner. I cannot follow their example and do the same without thinking of them the whole time."

"I find nothing makes amorous thoughts disappear faster than thinking of one's in-laws making love. I will try to hold back my baser instincts until after the entre' at least. Shall we go down now to prevent any back sliding on my part?" He put out his arm to guide Daisy up and out of the door.

Dinner was informal and all four people found themselves talking across the table as well as to their neighbor. Daisy's mother, most of her body hidden by the table, appeared more as an older sister than parent although it was agreed Lady Weatherly looked barely older than a debutante even now. William watched as mother and daughter conversed and laughed, sounding alike and happy to be with one another.

Daisy might have thought her previous life in this house had been as an outsider, but she was an integral piece of this family even though an adult piece. Daisy's father was also showing much pride in his daughter, not because she had captured a marquess, but because he thought her happy. William knew the man felt his daughter chose wisely and William wasn't going to disabuse the man of his beliefs.

It might have been with the help of Lady Reynolds that William was now married to Daisy, but it was due to his own tenacity she was his marchioness. He knew, somewhere deep inside, she was the right woman for him. That she would be the right mother for his children. It made it easier that Lady Reynolds had agreed, but given more time, he was sure he would have talked Daisy into accepting his offer. Even if he had to follow her home to Sussex to do so.

That night, snuggled in bed, William made love to his wife in a completely different manner. He was thinking her less of a wife and more of the mother of his child. He knew their lovemaking was a prerequisite for having a child together, but now he was more aware of everything that lovemaking represented. His commitment to Daisy as a husband, someone to care for her and be responsible for her in all things including her happiness and health.

Not simply make sure she had enough to eat and clothes to wear. He must support her emotionally, help her through her fears and stand beside her in all things.

To him that meant he must be with her, just as Lord Weatherly was with Lady Weatherly. Traveling back and forth to London would not have been enough for that man and William felt it would not be enough for him, either.

Perhaps, once Daisy is with child they would stay in the country for a few months. Then together, before she got too large for comfortable travel, they should move the household to London. That way she would be close to the best medical care and be surrounded by other ladies who could help her through the ordeal.

He knew after speaking with Lord Weatherly, William, too, would stay close throughout the confinement. There wasn't a power on earth strong enough to force him to leave Daisy's side until he was sure both she and the infant was safely delivered.

Possibly, after a few weeks, he could relax enough to allow her to venture out of the house but it would have to be mild weather and he would accompany her the first few times.

Pulling his wife closer to his body, he spooned her to his hips allowing his free hand to be splayed across her abdomen again, imagining his child pushing on it, flexing against the constraint of its weight. He brushed his lips across the top of Daisy's bare shoulder. He had not allowed her to re-dress after their lovemaking and now he had the added temptation of a naked wife in his bed and an active male member wanting to stake its claim once again.

Nudging Daisy's leg a little and true to form, his erection found the warm home it always sought. He entered her as she pushed her buttocks back into him, acknowledging his right to be there and her interest in his presence. She met his thrusts with her own pressure in return and his hand slid to her front to tease the nub growing alert with his attentions. It wasn't the heart-stopping release, but hopefully it would appease his own need so that he could allow them both to get some sleep.

Still, William stayed awake thinking, wondering at the change in himself. How he understood his in-laws so much better now. He had worried once Daisy was with child, she would no longer find a need for him to be in her bed. That he would once again be relegated to his own room with Vickers's critiquing every cravat and piece of lace in the clothes' press. Now he had no fear of being set aside. He pulled her closer once more as she settled in sleep for the remaining hours till the tea was brought.

He had to be truthful with himself. He loved his wife. Did not mean to love her, up to recently would have sworn no such emotion existed. That love of a man for a woman wasn't real. Maternal love was different and he had never seen any sign of paternal love so why would he look for it to happen to him?

He was now facing the fact he loved his wife after marrying her under the condition they not love one another. He thought the reason for marrying was expeditious of saving her reputation and keeping his own good name intact. Now he must wonder if he hadn't already felt more for Daisy than merely thinking she would make a good marchioness for him. Someone he would like to come home to in the country, someone to raise his children.

She was all those things as well.

CHAPTER NINE

Daisy's mother sat on the sofa, her hand on her protruding stomach as she watched her daughter pour tea. "Dearest, stop fussing and come and sit beside me. Your father rarely leaves me alone lately. I think he fears I will burst open if he walks out of the room."

"Mama, do not say such things. You know Father has always stayed close to you. I used to feel like an interloper sometimes and would go down to the kitchens so you would have the privacy you seemed to seek."

"We never meant for you to feel that way, dearest. You are our daughter, part of us, and part of our family just as this one will be."

"I understand and now I am married I understand why privacy is also important," she said hesitantly.

The viscountess watched her daughter closely and continued, "So now you know what is between a husband and wife? Are you in love with Lord Ashton then? Did you marry for love?"

"No, not at first. I was attracted to him. He is so handsome and he was so very nice to me when I almost gave up the idea of staying for the season. Even though I knew, Grandmother, would be hurt if I left so soon."

"But your feelings grew? Now you love him?" her mother asked anxiously.

"I think, I must. I mean I enjoy being with him and I will miss him once we get back to Ashton."

"So you are, let us use the term, compatible when you are intimate?"

Feeling her cheeks burn, Daisy said, "Mama, must we? I mean isn't this a little too much knowledge to share with one's parent?"

"No, this is exactly what one's parent should ask. I wish to know that you are happy, which you appear to be. That you are healthy, which except for being thinner, you appear to be. That you love and are loved...that is what I am trying to discern right now before the men come back and interrupt us."

"I didn't know how happy I actually would be when I agreed to marry William. Grandmother thought it best, of course, for various reasons but I merely wished to return home. I did not think William could be so caring. He is a good husband and I am grateful for Grandmother's and William's resolve in making me see that side of him."

"I am glad you will have the same love in your marriage as your father and I have found. I was worried we waited too long to send you to London for the season but we hated to lose you. We wished to keep you with us for as long as possible and then your grandmother insisted, we send you to her this year. My being with child was quite a shock, I must confess. I thank God, of course, but it meant we were unable to be with you in London."

"I do not think things would have been very different," Daisy said knowing she was misleading her mother. "I married the man of any debutante's dreams and I will live as a marchioness. I hope I will have the chance to be as good a mother as you are."

"Daisy, dearest, you will be much better than I was, I'm sure. This child will benefit from everything we learned raising you. I thought I should let the nanny and then the governess have control, but now I think I should have intervened more often. Spent time in the schoolroom with you, taken you to town to visit your grandmother to learn about London and the ton. It was how I was raised and I should have opened up the world to you, too."

"Mama, I do not regret missing out on town life or any other failure you think you were the cause of while I was growing up. It will seem odd for me to have a younger sibling, but I hope this child keeps both you and father feeling young and vital."

The lady looked at her daughter closely and asked, "Is there any chance this child will have an aunt or uncle soon? I would love to have our children grow up together. After all, we do not live that far from one another."

"I have no news to tell, but I agree the two children would make wonderful playmates and I could spend time here with you while William is in London." Daisy informed her mother while standing to pour more tea.

"William would leave you in Ashton while he went to stay in London? Are you speaking about a week or for months, Daisy?" her mother asked rather harshly.

"Um-m-m, I am not sure, Mama. I believe he likes to spend the season in town, whereas, I really prefer the country. It will not be a penance for me to stay at Ashton. Perhaps travel here, especially if I do not have children, yet." Trying to lighten the mood, she added, "I can practice on my sibling and you can teach me how to be as good a mother as you."

"Dearest, are you sure? Your father could have a talk with…."

Daisy quickly set her cup down and returned to the

sofa pleading, "I think the men are back from their ride. Please don't say anything to William. This is how the arrangement was made."

"If you are sure, dear. I do not like the idea of you being left alone in the country, though."

Daisy sat watching her image in the mirror. She did not look any different, nothing that showed in her face anyway, but she was changed. She was a woman now and, in many ways, widely more knowledgeable than what she was only a few weeks ago. Imagine if she had known then what she knew now. Would she have hesitated even an instant when William offered for her? Would she have argued with her grandmother or made those arrangements to leave town?

She would have more than likely compromised herself by throwing her naked body at Lord Ashton the first chance she got. Oh, no, he didn't think she had actually done such a thing, did he? She hadn't held anything back once they had become intimate. She reached out with both hands and grabbed what he offered. Grabbed it and did not let go.

Maybe she should have feigned a little modesty, a semblance of reserve instead of grasping his naked body to hers and moaning in ecstasy. But it was ecstasy. No wonder experienced women didn't impart knowledge about what happened between a man and a woman. The young woman would be throwing their hats over the windmills – several times a day. She blushed at her own thoughts.

Had William thought her too forward? Would he tell her if she asked or would he be kind to her, and say she was fine just as she was. He always insisted she would make a good marchioness, a good mother for his children, but that was before their first lovemaking. Did her enthusiasm to his intimate attentions make him turn from her in disgust afterwards? Would her actions make him think she wouldn't be a proper mother for his children?

He didn't mention the possibility of leaving her before conceiving his child. Was he planning on taking her back to Ashton and then continuing on to London for the weeks before the holidays? She was too unsure of her place in his life to feel free enough to ask. She hoped that she wouldn't be with child too soon or William would leave for London.

But she hadn't misled her mother, either. If William left for London, Daisy would return home to be with her parents.

CHAPTER TEN

A week to the day and Daisy found herself back at Ashton. The two-day return trip went quickly and she and William talked more. Daisy was searching for ways in which they agreed and had been pleasantly surprised to find how often their thinking matched.

"You think a child should be in their parent's rooms, especially as an infant?" Daisy asked almost thinking she misheard her husband.

"I think a mother and infant should remain close, yes. They have just shared a body. Why, all of a sudden, should they be separated by walls and doors and several other people. Do you think you want an army of nursemaids between you and our child?"

"My mother and I were discussing this very thing. I spent the first year in a cradle next to my parent's bed. Of course, I was unaware of it but Mama insists this next child will be treated the same. They have a nurse, but Mama took care of me through the night and wishes to do the same this time. She slept during the day and the nursemaid or my father cared for me." Then she teased, "How are you with a nappy?"

Shooting his cuff, he said dryly, "I am sure I can handle anything a nursery maid can."

"I would beware of what I said if I were you, my lord. Infants can be very messy beings. I may not have siblings yet, but I did have some experience with small children in the church."

"Then I will depend on you teaching me what I will

need to know. If your father could do so, I will care for my child as well."

The servants showed appreciative emotion upon their return to Ashton and Daisy felt welcomed, even though she had been their marchioness for such a short time. Evidently these people missed the feminine portion of their titled family.

The housekeeper brought up the Christmas Eve festivities of years past, when William's mother was still alive. There had always been a sort of celebration prior to the church services. The invited villagers and tenant farmers came to the manor for refreshments and then sang carols on their way to the village church. Daisy thought she should renew the tradition and set plans in motion for the coming Christmas Eve whether her husband was with her or not.

William entered his wife's room wearing his banyan saying, "You spent a long time with the housekeeper today. No problems are there?"

Daisy picked up her brush as she explained, "We were working on the holidays. Resurrecting one of the traditions now you have a marchioness for a hostess. I was going to make sure you were in agreement before I confirmed the plans."

"I remember them. I was often away on Christmas Eve with friends but I think we should bring back some of the traditions. It is a way to celebrate for all of Ashton and the village."

"That is what I thought and Mrs. Higgins thought it would go over well with everyone. I will speak with the vicar to make sure there are no problems there," Daisy said as she climbed into the bed.

William joined her after dropping his banyan and sliding between the sheets naked up against her muslin gown. He reached for her and pulled her close.

"Is there anything you want to tell me besides household news? Like whether I am to get the cradle ready for our little one?"

Flustered, Daisy stammered, "I, ah, I do not know for sure. I thought I should wait before saying anything. It has not been that long and…."

He moved her body so that he could put his arms around her. "I'm sorry, Daisy. I guess I am merely anxious after seeing your mother and imagining you carrying my child. I do not mean to rush you. If it does not happen right away that should mean we keep trying," he whispered into her ear.

"Yes, I guess we should keep trying," she said weakly knowing that she probably already carried his child but wasn't ready for him to leave her yet. Not ready to admit how much she would miss him.

"Then we should take pleasure in one another. I enjoy making love to you every night and I have no intention of stopping until you tell me I must."

After their lovemaking, Daisy could not sleep as she usually did, knowing she would not be able to hide her condition much longer. If William knew anything about women, he would know she had not had her courses. She would need to become used to his leaving her.

She would run his home and raise his child and appreciate everything he did for her when he was at home. If he spent time at home. She was a marchioness and her life was dictated by her husband. She knew that when she had accepted his offer of marriage.

At least she liked him, admittedly loved him, and she would learn to live without his constant presence once he was gone. She would have her babe to worry over and eventually William would come and live with her again when he wished to add to the nursery. In many ways, she was blessed and having a husband as devoted as her father was to her mother was a rarity and not meant for a marchioness.

Alice and James Wainwright arrived days after Daisy's return from her parents. The butler announced them as she sat in the summer room crocheting.

Lady Alice rushed in all bows and ribbons and lace smelling of roses. James entered in a more dignified manner, but both chose to lean in and kiss Daisy as a sister more than a friend, which put Daisy to the blush. She and Alice wrote to one another but Daisy felt she had burned her boats in London.

The siblings took a seat on a matching sofa opposite Daisy. "You look wonderful, Daisy, dear. You must come back to town soon and show those old tabbies what a real marchioness looks like. How dare they turn up their noses at you," Alice said almost before she sat down.

"Lady Alice, you can hardly blame them. I came out of nowhere and then Wil, I mean, Lord Ashton, paid so much attention to me. I am sure there were many disappointed mothers out there. I, for one, was completely surprised when my lord offered for me." Daisy tried minimalizing the sensationalism of her hasty marriage to the marquess.

James added, "Come now, Daisy, er, my lady, all of us fellows were trying to gain your attention. We just hadn't realized our competition was so strong. A marquess is difficult to best."

Alice interrupted saying, "It does not matter now. Everyone that bet on those duke's daughters lost their money and I for one am not the least bit sorry for them. It was horrible the way people tried to get the marquess interested in one or the other of those poor girls." Alice gave her brother a glare only a sister could give. "But we need not concern ourselves with that any longer, my lady. We are here for a short visit so I can assure you, in person, we hold you in the highest regard."

Daisy was glad to see her old friends, perhaps her only friends from London. "Please, let us go back to using our Christian names as we did in town. I am not used to being my lady yet and especially not from my friends."

James bowed slightly. "As you wish, Daisy."

Alice added, "Of course. I have trouble remembering you are a marchioness although I always thought that Lord Ashton was interested in you. I think Lady Reynolds knew, also. I used to see them talking quietly at every event. And the way the marquess looked at you when you waltzed. That was unmistakably love."

Embarrassed now, Daisy began talking quickly, "Well, I am glad you could come for a visit. Are you able to stay for a while? I have not had anyone come except for the local vicar and his wife. A few of the local landowners' wives have come for tea."

"I know it is not the done thing to come uninvited, but James and I were returning from a cousin's wedding. I have written more than once threatening to visit if you were not returning to London to finish the season. It was not out of the way by much," Alice finished lamely.

"You are both more than welcome. I would have

been saddened to learn you had been nearby and felt you could not stop. We have plenty of rooms and James can fill Ashton in on what is happening in London. He usually only gets letters from his man of business or lawyers. Nothing about what is really occurring. Like who bought what horse, the kind of things men speak of at the clubs. I think Wil...Ashton misses his club the most."

"I would be happy to accommodate, his lordship. I belong to at least one of the same clubs and as to keeping track of the horse flesh, I do not brag when I say no one gets new stock that I am unaware of."

William entered still wearing his riding breeches and put out a hand to James, saying, "I thought I heard voices. How nice of you to come for a visit. I fear Daisy is growing bored with the place now we have returned from visiting her parents. Not much entertainment and only myself to talk with in the evenings."

"My lady has not complained a bit so I must assume she is as blissfully happy as she assures us, she is," James said gallantly.

"Daisy is not one to complain, but I found her so much more loquacious with her parents. I am thinking of taking her back to town when I go," William said aloud for the first time to Daisy's confusion. She thought she had been delegated to the country, but now her husband was announcing to others he was thinking of taking her with him.

The teacart arrived with small sandwiches and bottles of sherry and Madeira. Daisy relaxed as she took over her duties as hostess. After the extended tea, everyone went to his or her rooms to rest and then dress for dinner. Alice made a quick request to speak with

Daisy once things settled down to which Daisy acquiesced easily.

The cook made a festive meal, knowing visitors are to be treated special and Daisy felt pride that her staff was up to every aspect of a London staff, even if they kept country hours.

James kept them all entertained with his antidotes of people they all knew or were aware of in society. He was witty and droll and charming. Daisy thought she might have made a match with him if William had not entered the scene and become so much a part of her life.

After dinner, the men went to the billiard room although Daisy hadn't even known of its existence while Alice and Daisy spent time in the family parlor.

Alice could hardly wait for the men to leave. "I was hoping we could have some time alone. I wished to tell you what has happened after you left town and you will consider me a gossip or worse, I am sure, but I think you should know these things."

"Alice, I do not think you a gossip or you would have spilled my antics when you had the chance, yet, you did not. What is it you feel you need to unburden your soul by telling me?"

"Firstly, Lady Gannon left right after you did using the excuse she was going to need as much time as she could to plan the wedding. That it had to be done from their country home since that is where the wedding was to be held," Alice confided as if it were a secret elopement. "But the groom stayed in town and proceeded to get drunk every night and frequent houses of, let us say, friendly women of less than pristine reputations."

Daisy told her friend, "Many young men seem to

feel the need to sow their wild oats or some such thing when facing a wedding. And that wedding seemed to have been arranged quickly although I should not speak of such things since mine was also done immodestly fast."

"Yes, and the whole ton knew that was so your grandmother could be witness to the event and be able to die easier knowing you were well cared for. No one was shocked at the special license. We were all glad she lived to see her hopes and dreams accomplished. All the older people of society knew of her desires for you and had been helping her with her plans. How do you think all those invitations arrived just as you were thinking of leaving?"

Daisy went over the past season in her mind and nodded, "I can see that she must have pulled in even more favors than I first assumed. She didn't have anything on William, did she?"

"No, you goose. That was all due to you. He was smitten. Everyone who watched you dance together could tell he was attracted to you. My money would have been on you from the beginning. That is, if I placed a bet, which you discouraged me from doing right from the start," Alice added hastily.

"I still disagree with that thinking, but I know I was flattered and appreciative of what his attention had done for me. The doors it opened and how much Grandmother relaxed after he showed some regard. I will forever be grateful because it did make the last few weeks of my grandmother's life easier."

"Back to the other. It seems that Lady Gannon's daughter is with child and the wedding has already taken place quietly. All those still waiting for an invitation will be waiting a long time. No one wishes to be on that lady's wrong side so talk is subdued but I thought you should know. Her daughter was not marchioness material either, it seems, so the lady will not be speaking about you at any time."

Watching Daisy closely, Alice said, "I know what she said seemed to make an impact on you, but it didn't on the rest of us. You always held yourself away from the gossips and the tattlers and the rest of us know that is the true sign of a lady. Someone deserving of becoming a marchioness or a duchess, if one wished. I wish you to know that when you come back to London, you will have nothing to fear. You will be welcomed with open arms by the hostesses and Ashton will take second fiddle to you."

William entered smiling followed by James. "Did I hear my name taken in vain? Can I not leave the room before you two are tearing me to shreds over some simple misstep? New husbands are allowed a few errors, but I would eagerly make up for any blunder if I am told what I did wrong."

"Not a thing wrong, husband. Simply catching up with boring town goings on. I assure you we missed nothing in leaving the season early," Daisy said knowing she wouldn't tell him about the other news she heard. It was old and she found no effect on her life as she lived it now.

The sister and brother stayed two days, but then found they were due to attend a last of the season's ball before parliament broke for the holidays. James had promised the young lady concerned the first waltz.

Alice confided, "I think James is more smitten than he would let on. I like the young lady, too, so it wouldn't be onerous to have her join the family."

Blushing, James said, "Whoa there. Do not say such things in public or you will have me leg-shackled in no time. Some of these eager mammas do not need much to have a ring in my nose before there is a ring on the chit's finger."

Daisy raised her hand up in protest. "No more. Say no more then. I will wait to hear any announcement just as the rest of the world does, perhaps a few days later since the newspapers arrive by post."

James replied, his color still high, "I can assure you that there will not be an announcement this year. I will stop dancing with anyone if my sister insists on speaking of such things."

"All right, brother dear, I will restrain myself but that does not mean some of us ladies do not have our pin money bet on a certain lady who shall remain unnamed as your intended."

Looking towards Ashton for support, James asked of no one in particular, "Has anyone been so besieged in their life by their own sibling? There are times I wish I were an only child."

CHAPTER ELEVEN

Several days after their guests left, William was lying next to his wife and said confidently, "I think we should return to town for the end of the season. I know you are still in half-mourning but we should be able to attend the dinners and final festivities. I will refrain from asking you to waltz." He kissed her ear and nipped her neck with his lips.

Daisy tensed and let out a breath. "I need to tell you something before you make a decision like that. I am with child and you need not stay at Ashton with me any longer. I will wait here until the child is born and you can decide what I should do after that."

Seemingly ecstatic, William hugged her closer and whispered in awe, "I was beginning to suspect it but I was waiting for you to confirm my suspicions. I am so happy, dearest, I truly am.

"Of course, we won't travel now. We will stay here and have even more reasons to celebrate Christmas and the New Year. I will be a father come summer, right? Do I have it correct?" William kissed his wife and wrapped her close as if she would disappear from their own bed if he allowed her any space.

"I thought you wished to go to London once I was with child. You know, get back with your friends and your clubs. Read news when it can still be called news. I do not need you beside me the entire time. The baby will not be here for months."

"Of course, I am staying with you. I cannot have you

traveling in this bad weather and possibly get stuck on the road somewhere. And I cannot leave you. Nothing is more important to me than you and my child. I will not leave either."

"But you said...I thought you wished to leave once your duty was over."

"You make it sound so cold blooded, dearest. I was new to the marriage and didn't understand how I would feel about becoming a father. I find I like the idea quite well and I like being a husband just as much. I think the plans for the holiday will still be able to take place, but we will take things easier toward spring. I cannot see us visiting your mother after the birth of your sibling, but perhaps they can travel to us after a couple of months."

"You must have been thinking of this for a while, William, if you even have the summer planned out for me," Daisy was amazed at his change of plans. "When did you change your mind about leaving me and allowing me to give birth alone at Ashton."

"I don't know when I changed my mind. Possibly when we visited your parents and I realized I wanted to see you large with my child, feel him or her kick me, talk to my child while it's still in your womb. I want to know my child and let my child know me. Do you think I am quite mad?" He was smiling widely, his manner more enthusiastic than she had ever seen him.

"No, not quite mad, not yet, but I fear you may become a little controlling as I do get larger. I think perhaps you and my father had too many heart-to-heart talks. He has convinced you that this is what you should do, too."

"I watched your father, both your parents, and I did make up my mind that I wanted what they have. I'm going to stay with you and my child. I will not be a stranger who meets with my child once a week or once a month or only at term breaks."

"That is exactly what I wish as well, husband. I will write my mother to let her know about our child and to explain why I will not be able to be by her side."

Daisy looked up at her husband beseechingly. "Unless you think I can do the short trip there before Christmas?"

"I am afraid not. The roads are too risky in December and we have all those plans for the end of the month. I do not want you over-doing things. You are too precious."

Daisy snuggled against her husband and agreed. "Yes, I may be carrying the next marquess."

The letter Daisy was waiting for finally arrived one morning while she and William were still breaking their fast. She opened it excitedly and squealed with delight.

"I have a brother, William. Mama finally gave Father an heir. They must both be ecstatic. I must write back and wish them all the best. I hardly know what all to say. I so wish I could have gone and stayed with them."

"I know, dearest, but it could just as soon of been later in the month and you would not have wanted to return to Ashton for the festivities. The roads are muddy, even now, without any sign of a freeze to make them passable. I think this was the best plan."

"I have to agree and Mama tells me I am not to try to visit until after I have delivered. In fact, she will be sending me her midwife since she thinks the woman is highly skilled and well experienced. The woman will arrive early, as soon as Mama is no longer in need of her and she will act as nurse if we need, also."

Daisy picked up the sheet of folded paper and scanned the lines again. "Mama has brought back my nursery maid to help with little, Arthur. So, my brother is to be named after my father. How wonderful for all of them. I wish I had been there."

"It sounds as if they will be able to travel here before you will travel there. It will be almost the same and safer for you and our child. I was worried about us being here and not closer to London and the medical professionals, but if your mother thinks this midwife is good then I think we can leave you in her capable hands as well."

Daisy watched as Christmas Eve was celebrated in the old traditions of Ashton Manor with everyone gathering in the ballroom for holiday fare. Children received mittens and hats and the women received knit shawls. Mrs. Higgins, the housekeeper, received one that Daisy crocheted for her and Higgins received a crocheted muffler. The rest of the men got a pair of socks and a coin. The group was very merry as they caroled to the village and the midnight service.

After the first of the year, William put off all thoughts of travel. She knew he wrote to let his friends know not to expect him back to town this coming season, but invited them to come to visit if they felt the need to see him. He told her he would definitely remain by her side until after the birth of his daughter or heir.

Daisy's life returned to a normal routine, but was no longer allowed to ride out with her husband in the mornings when he checked his fields and tenants. They broke their fast together, then spent most of the afternoon in the library writing letters or reading to one another.

"What have you got there, dearest?" William looked at the torn sheets of paper in her hands.

"Mother sent some patterns for infant clothes and suggestions as to what I will need. She wrote that when the midwife, McClellan, arrives she will be a help, also. I think I will look for fabric in the linen closet." She scurried out toward the stairs and William waited in the library for her to return.

At night, they slept in the same bed just as they had before. After being assured it was safe, William made love to her nightly as they were used to doing.

Daisy was more relaxed than she had been in her life. She would not allow her worries to intrude on her happiness, would not let doubts of her husband's contentment needle at her, would not allow herself to think of William's attention to the baby would somehow lessen what she felt they had together.

Mrs. McClellan arrived and took over the nursery which covered most of the third floor. That included the nursemaids' rooms, separate quarters for a nanny which McClellan usurped, the infant's sleeping room, the extra rooms for older children, the classroom and play area.

That woman began to set up the nursery as well as making a list of things Daisy would need for the infant. Even more extensive than her mother's. How did one baby need all those items?

Daisy did not argue but instead retrieved her crochet needles and began more sweaters and dresses with matching booties. She was either going to have the best dressed infant or a fine start of a layette for her next child.

William was content. Without realizing it, he had

become the type of marquess he was unable to picture himself as before. He took time to listen to his tenants, he allowed his steward more say in how to best use the lands and woods, and he spent an inordinate amount of time with his wife.

After calling his married friends all sorts of provocative names for wanting to be with their spouses, William was as guilty of wishing to be home in the evenings with Daisy. They played billiards, or read to one another or argued politics. He came to understand his wife more and began to understand her childhood, as well.

Daisy wanted a marriage like her parents had or not have one at all. It wasn't about title or money or power. She was raised to think of those things as being unimportant. To her, marriage was more than a merging of two families or even two bodies. It was centered on two hearts.

He stole that dream from her when he selfishly put his own wants and wishes above hers. He didn't know how to change that fact, but he could make sure she didn't regret the marriage or the child she was carrying.

He never told her, but he thought he loved his wife. He didn't want her to feel badly for not reciprocating the emotion. After all, it had been William who assured her that love was over-rated when it came to marriage. That, in fact, it didn't even exist. He now realized how wrong he had been. He could only hope that eventually she would find more than the affection he thought she felt for him.

Sharing this time in their lives brought him such joy, such peace. He found his hand on her stomach every morning recently waiting for his child to bump him as it woke from the night's rest. His heart swelled with emotion for something he had never met yet. Someone who would be part of his universe which had them both circling Daisy like planets to the sun.

McClellan, the midwife, was very vocal of her patient's needs and very vocal about what he should be doing or rather not doing with his wife any longer. He wasn't happy with her edict, but knew the woman was only protecting Daisy and his unborn child. He remained sleeping with his wife - just not sleeping with his wife. He thought he would have several weeks of this benign torture.

His butler's shouting brought him to the house after his morning ride to be told his wife was laying in and that he would be notified once the child was born.

But this was too soon. The midwife put the confinement date into July and it was barely June. He and Daisy knew the possibility of her getting pregnant prior to October was impossible. They postponed their consummation due to her grandmother's death and then traveling. William could almost smell the scent of the lemon syllabub that day was so imprinted in his mind.

The date could not be wrong and that meant the baby was early. He wished he had asked more questions of the midwife. He remembered her saying babies had their own sense of time, but did that mean they always knew when it was safe to be born? Would Daisy be safe and what would she do if she lost this child?

He knew she was content to stay with him as long as she was carrying their child, but if she lost it would she leave him? Return to her parents and live as a single woman? Would she still seek to find a man to love?

William didn't want to think of those complications.

Perhaps this was a mistake, perhaps the baby wasn't actually ready to be born and this was some sort of trial or practice for the actual birth.

After several hours, William knew that all his scenarios were false. His wife was going to give birth over a month early and he would need to be strong for her in case the child didn't make it. He never wished for Daisy's parent's presence more than now. Her father would stabilize him and her mother would be the consolation Daisy would need if the child didn't make it.

William didn't want to think about the outcome if Daisy didn't make it. He would not even think of a world without her in it, without her breathing air somewhere on earth. This then was when the prayers began.

He tried to pray but found himself feeling selfish, he couldn't trade one life for another, one love for another. He would need to be strong for her and he would not think about Daisy leaving him either through death or if the child didn't live. He would have to believe that his wife would give their marriage another chance, that she would still want children.

William stood with his forehead pressed to the door, both hands pushing against it to keep him from swinging it open and storming into the room. He heard the sounds from inside the room. Moans and groans, the muffled cries of agony. He was impotent to keep his wife from the pain. That he was the direct cause of that pain ate at him with guilt. He never thought about what giving birth would mean to Daisy, never dreamt he would feel so useless now when the time faced them both.

He fisted his hands but did not pound the wood, as he wanted to do, did not bring pain to himself while upsetting his wife with his antics. He hated being locked out but feared that his interruption of the process would bring more pain and possibly even be dangerous to Daisy and the child. He would need to be as brave as his little wife and bear her moans and whimpers of pain with as much fortitude as she was.

He remembered everything the midwife had explained to him, much of it in graphic detail. He had asked, wanted, needed, to know what Daisy was going to experience. Lord Weatherly said that when Daisy was born, it was the worst thing for him to go through knowing he was the cause of his wife's pain. William remembered thinking then - how much pain could there be? After all, it was a natural process and he had witnessed horses giving birth and they stood-up afterwards and the foal stood-up within minutes.

How stupid must he be to think that it was anything like the same for a woman – his woman. McClellan told him that he would want to try to take some of the pain from his wife, but he didn't understand exactly how strong that desire became. He would do anything to lessen Daisy's suffering, anything at this point, any promise, any bargain with the devil.

A wail was heard muffled through the door and William's heart leaped into his throat. His hand went to the doorknob but he held himself back. He would not intrude until McClellan called him, until Daisy could face him after what he had made her go through. The silence was louder than any clap of thunder. Shouldn't there be more noise or more elation that it was all over?

Daisy's drawn out cry of pain had William whipping the door open in frustration as he raced around the bed to his wife's side ignoring the shocked faces of the housekeeper and Daisy's maid. He clasped Daisy's hand as her body lifted from the pillow, her damp hair clinging to her face, perspiration beading on her brow. Suddenly he realized how much blood was on the bed and sheets and the gown she was wearing.

McClellan ignored him and his uninvited presence, once more having her attention riveted to the private place between his wife's legs and cooing encouraging words to Daisy.

William was at a loss as to what to do or how to help now that he was there. Molly, he realized, held a small bundle that she was rocking slowly side to side so what was the problem with Daisy.

Daisy once again stiffened and leaned forward. Clutching his hand with such force he knew he winced, but knowing it was probably nothing to the amount of pressure and pain his wife was enduring stoically.

She flopped back in relief and another angry howl rent the air as a wet, messy infant was retrieved in a small blanket and once more a bundle was being shushed and wrapped tightly. Mrs. Higgins took that one from the midwife.

McClellan paid no more attention to the babies, all her attention on Daisy, all her attention on the woman he loved.

William paid attention only to his wife also, making sure she was still awake and would hear what had taken him too long to say, "I love you, Daisy, please don't leave me. I love you, only you."

Daisy patted his hand almost too exhausted to speak but got out, "I know, my darling, I know. You are more like my father than I realized."

As he put his head down next to Daisy's on the pillow, McClellan's bold, blunt orders interrupted him.

"My lord, ye ha' to get up now so we can clean-up m'lady and give her the bairns for a bit."

He looked pleadingly to his wife, "May I stay? I won't get in the way, I promise."

McClellan barked out to the housekeeper, "Gie him one of the bairns then and that will keep him busy a while. Ye have two daughters, by the way, exactly alike. I don't envy you in 'bout eighteen years when they off and marry."

Mrs. Higgins handed her bundle to him and although he held it oddly, he was in awe of the tiny face that peered out at him. Dark eyes, pansy eyes he was sure, looking up at him. He turned away, feeling his own eyes fill with tears and communed with his second born daughter. It was so much a miracle he was hard pushed to believe he had any part in her being there. Moreover, there was still another he had yet to be introduced to. It was such a momentous, emotional time.

William lay on the top of the bed waiting for Daisy to waken naturally. Knowing she was exhausted from the birth, knowing she could be angry with him when she did finally wake, he was anxious to share this time with her. He didn't care how much she might rail at him. He could not leave her, them because both babies were nestled in the cradle together, heads at either end until a second cradle could be built.

He saw Daisy's eyes open slowly and saw the smile creep across her face. "I am sorry that I did not have your heir. The pressure would have been off you, if I had."

"I feel no pressure. I have two beautiful daughters who will have their mother's violet pansy eyes and I am so blessed I cannot hold my heart in my chest. I do not know how to express myself. Only that I understand what your parents have. I now understand how two people can wish to be together every moment of every day."

Then quieter, he whispered, "I understand the need to make love to one's wife even when one is old, when one has children of twenty years because even at this moment I cannot fathom a time when I will not want to be joined with you."

"Did no one ever explain to you that it was bad form to speak about love making to a woman who has just given birth?"

"Add it to my list of faux pas for the day, dearest. I think the entire village knows by now that I entered the birthing room without being invited and that I cried like a baby over my daughters," he told her slightly abashed.

"And I love you for doing both, my husband. I would not have it any other way. You made the second birth easier. I cannot explain it. I was at ease the moment I felt your hand in mine. Anything that felt so right cannot be wrong."

"Then I will hold my head up and dare anyone to question my right to be there with you."

"And I will confide something McClellan told me. My father was with my mother the entire time. From the first twinge of pain until their child was born, both times. He was the first to hold me after I was born, the first one to gaze into my eyes, and the first to talk to me as I heard you do with our daughters."

"I have been singing to them since I thought they could hear me. They should love to waltz when they get older," he teased now that Daisy seemed stronger and more awake. "I love you and I do not care if it is not the tonish thing to do. I love my wife and I no longer care who else knows it."

"That is all we can wish for, then. Although I have a feeling there will be more children in our future. I have what I need out of life."

"As do I, wife, as do I." William kissed Daisy and held her close. So thankful he decided to hide behind that blessed palm.

A word about the author...

A voracious reader her whole life, author Susan Payne loved the written word. When reading more than fifty books per month wasn't enough, she decided to allow her mind to take flight and write all the many stories that kept intruding into her life. She blended her love of history and her love of words to create over eighty stories. All historical and centering on a couple finding love and a happy ever after together.

You may contact Susan at:
http://www.authorsusanpayne.com or
authorspayne@gmail.com

Thank you for purchasing
this publication of The Wild Rose Press, Inc.

For questions or more information
contact us at
info@thewildrosepress.com.

The Wild Rose Press, Inc.
www.thewildrosepress.com

www.ingramcontent.com/pod-product-compliance
Lightning Source LLC
Chambersburg PA
CBHW071813200626
46813CB00020B/1724